Exiled

Memoirs of a Camel

BY Kathleen Karr

Marshall Cavendish

Copyright ©2004 by Kathleen Karr

Marshall Cavendish Corporation, 99 White Plains Road, Tarrytown, NY 10591

www.marshallcavendish.us

Library of Congress Cataloging-in-Publication Data

Karr, Kathleen.

Exiled : memoirs of a camel / by Kathleen Karr.—1st Marshall Cavendish
paperback ed.

p. cm.

Summary: In the nineteenth century, Ali the camel is separated from his mother
in Egypt and sent to Texas, where he becomes part of the United States Camel
Corps, but does not forget his longing for sand dunes and freedom.

ISBN-13: 978-0-7614-5291-1 (pbk.)

ISBN-10: 0-7614-5291-5 (pbk.)

ISBN-10: 0-7614-5164-1 (hardcover)

1. United States. Army. Camel Corps—History—Juvenile fiction. [1. United
States. Army. Camel Corps--History—Fiction. 2. Camels—Southwestern
States—History—Fiction. 3. Texas—History—19th century—Fiction. 4.
Mojave Desert (Calif.)—Fiction.] I. Title.

PZ7.K149Ex 2006

[Fic]—dc22

2005022342

The text of this book is set in Lapidary 333.

Book design by Anahid Hamparian

Printed in the United States of America

First Marshall Cavendish paperback edition, 2006

2 4 6 8 10 9 7 5 3

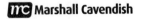

** mc Marshall Cavendish**

For Tracey Adams
—who loved Ali from the moment
she met him

Exile

*Do they not look
at the Camels,
How they are made?*

LXXXVIII, 17
QUR'AN

One

Allah in His infinite wisdom created my kind, and I have no grudge to bear on that account. Are we not full of His meaning and high design? Are not we Ships of the Desert wonderfully practical? We can survive without water for days. We can live on thorns. But the part about carrying men and goods, and having hair useful for weaving, and flesh that can be eaten . . . truly this I could have done without. I also could have done without exile from my native land. But that, after all, is the meat and drink of my story.

❖ ❖ ❖

When I was born on the banks of the Upper Nile near Luxor, no mountains shook to proclaim my destiny. Yet the great Nile flooded that very day. My mother, prodding me on my wobbly legs from harm's way, offered the first intimations of my future.

"Ali," she said, "your father was a prince among camels. He ran faster through the desert than any other. He bowed to no man. Praise be to Allah, you will grow to his stature."

I tried then and there to raise my long neck to a height worthy of my noble father. Mother wickered gently.

"In time, Ali. You will find your true bearing in time. For now try to understand that the destiny of our kind has always been tied to man—as this land is tied to the Nile, Mother of All Rivers. When the river moves, we move. When man threatens, we yield."

"Yield? Not me!" I snorted.

Mother shook her head in amusement. "You are very young, my son. You will learn to bend without stooping. Only remember one thing—"

"What thing, Mother?"

"An important thing. We camels have never submitted willingly. Should you be taken by the two-legged beasts, recall this. Work, but never surrender." Then she nuzzled me tenderly and let me at her teats.

My milk days were peaceful. I followed my mother as she grazed in the ruins of the Ancient Ones at Karnak. How often she paused next to a vast column—as wide as a camel's length and taller than twenty of us— and spoke to me of the mysteries pictured on the stone. There were connections, she said. Connections between those pictures and hieroglyphs and our honorable past.

There was a broken line in the memories of men, but we camels remembered.

Some of it was hard for me to grasp before I began to use my grazing teeth, yet I liked the pictures—and the colors, too, even worn and softened as they were. Besides, the shade was cool beneath the broken roofs of times past. But questions came to me.

"Why are we not painted onto this stone, Mother, as the donkeys are?"

"The donkeys submitted first, Ali. Our submission was never completed. Have I ever nuzzled a man-beast as I nuzzle you? No. First, I will bite the hand that cares for me. It is ordained."

I thought long and hard over these things as we spent tranquil days among the ruins. I also took more note of the statues lining long paths between the columns. The men-beast shapes were very large and grand.

Still . . . they were always missing one necessary thing.

"Mother? How do the men-beasts breathe without noses? Thus far you have shielded me from the real ones, but these images . . ."

Mother gave her rumbling laugh. It was always very deep and comforting. "Menbeasts are a strange race in more ways than one, Ali. They are never satisfied with the bounty Allah has given them but always seek more. In seeking more, they rarely hesitate to harm one of their own."

She nodded toward the figures. "Those statues have no noses because other men have destroyed them. It is their belief that such defacing will keep an enemy from enjoying the Gardens of Heaven."

I stopped looking to pull a soothing sip from my mother's teat. "He who would keep another from the glories of Heaven must be very mean indeed."

"Alas, Ali. It is so."

In my tenth moon my mother went dry, and I had to console myself with the power of my young teeth on the thorn brush. The taste was not as sweet as my mother's milk, but there was much thorn, and it was filling.

It was in my eleventh moon that the first terrible event of my life occurred. Grazing one day behind Karnak's Temple of Amun-Re, where we had always felt safe and protected, my mother and I were captured by men-beasts. Mother fought ferociously with her teeth and her legs. I watched, learned, and put up a fair fight myself. It was not enough. The men-beasts were too many. Soon there was a rope around my neck, and we were being led to a place I'd never seen outside the town of Luxor.

I tried to walk next to my mother, and

she gave me what final comfort and advice she could.

"They will take us to a camel market, Ali. I have seen them before. Remember all I have taught you. But—" She stopped as she struggled with the thought. "But if we must be parted, I pray Allah will care for you, my son, and give you an honorable life."

"Mother—"

Too late. I was jerked away viciously and received the first taste of the man-beast's true nature: fierce blows upon my rear quarters. I looked for a hand to bite, but they were all well out of harm's way. Never mind. There would be many hands to bite in my future.

The camel market appeared out of a haze shimmering beneath the sharp blue of the sky. It was in a dry wadi surrounded by a few date palms. The smells from this gully were strange and distressful—odors of many humans and much smoke. As we came closer, I could see men-beasts swathed in their *gallibiyas* and turbans seated everywhere, nearly all smoking the bubbling water pipes they called *hookahs*. I closed my nose flap as my mother had taught me to do during sandstorms. Even then the stench came through. I kicked out and was rewarded with more blows.

The blows made me very angry.

With one strong lunge, I pulled the rope from my tormentor's hands, leaped through the jumble of men-beasts, and loped off east to the desert beyond. I ran faster than I had ever run before. And the faster I ran, the stronger I felt. Perhaps I had my father's blood after all. Jubilant with this thought, I raced with a passion, forgetting my pursuers.

They did not forget me. Riders on older

camels followed, and soon I was surrounded.

I looked upon my elders balefully. "Traitors!"

"Young fool," grumbled the nearest bull, "now you'll be in for it!"

Back at the market I paid for my folly. My escape had merely raised my price among the men-beasts. Now they looked on me with interest in their eyes. Perhaps I could become a racer, they speculated. Thus was I quickly sold under my mother's eyes. Thus was I led off again—protesting fiercely, impotently—toward the great Nile. My mother's roar of pain followed me.

"Remember, Ali. Remember!"

The Mother of All Rivers had given me drink, but never had I ventured upon her waters. I was prodded onto a felucca, one of the sailing ships of the river, and transported to the side of the setting sun. Once there

I had no wish to set foot upon the earth. Was not the West the land of death?

My mother had explained this to me. West was the place of burials. Here the Ancients waited with their belongings in tombs. Waited for Heaven to find their ka-souls.

Humph. All very well for the Ancients. But I, Ali, was not ancient. I had no wish to sample this mystery.

The men-beasts should have understood. They should have understood my anguish over being torn from my mother, too. Instead, they beat me more harshly than ever.

Enough.

I spun. Snapped at a hand. Found my teeth and tongue enveloping fingers for the first time. Discovered the salty taste.

Crunched.

The man-beast howled.

I leaped for the shore and waited for doom to overtake me. The doom of the dead Ancients. The doom of these too alive men-beasts. Shivering through the heat, I turned my back on the West and faced the boat, the river, my tormentors—every defense at the ready.

No doom. *Nothing.* The injured man-beast merely wrapped his hand in a filthy rag—and kept a healthy distance from me.

Hah. I tossed my head and pawed the sandy ground. A lesson learned. I'd have to think about its meaning.

For more than a year I stayed on that particular western bank of the Nile learning the differences between *yield* and *submit*. Working out those subtleties helped ease my silent mourning for my mother. Slowly her spirit merged into special places within my head and my heart where I could find her and her wisdom when I needed succor. Thus I learned strength, if not always judgment.

Two

The men-beasts were waiting for me to develop before they raced me. While I grew, they trained me to carry burdens. It was a very distasteful process. Granted, they bided their time until my twelfth moon, but that maturing accomplished, they proceeded with relish.

First, they painfully pierced my nose and placed a wooden bit through the new openings.

While my nose was still tender with healing, they marked my neck with a burning hot iron. I was given the thin, diagonal stripes that I had seen on my mother—the stripes that marked my breed, *Mahazi of Bechaniah*. I bore this pain well, for I knew it was an honor to be of this clan. We carried our necks high and proudly, and had the smoothest trot and the fastest run of any dromedary.

Yet hardly had I recovered from these shocks when new outrages began.

One morning I was forced to the ground in my sleeping position. A moth-eaten blanket was thrown over my back and hump. Next, stones were piled upon this blanket. In days to come, stones were added in ever increasing weights. I fought each addition, but as my legs were tied beneath me, I could do little harm to the master. I could but lie there, groaning beneath the despised burden. Having much time to think during these hours, I plotted all manner of retribution to those beasts who would tame me to their needs. My teeth and tongue were always ready for another salty taste of man.

I looked to the graybeards in the herd for counsel but learned these elders were undoubtedly of lesser breeding. For one thing, they merely laughed at my hateful period of training.

"We all have passed through the same apprenticeship, Ali. No camel goes through life untamed and untrained. It is an honor to carry burdens upon our strong backs."

"Honor, *pah*!" I spat at the very idea. "My father carried no burdens. He raced free—like the wind—and someday so shall I!"

"*Princeling*." Scorn tinged the word. "Someday you will grow up and learn your place."

I staunchly ignored all such counsel.

These camels knew nothing of dreams. They knew nothing of their noble heritage. They knew nothing of revenge. Only look what happened when the master angered them! The master would remove his ragged *gallibiya*, toss it on the ground, and hastily make his retreat. My elders then proceeded to kick, stomp, and spit upon the robe until their ire was sated. That accomplished, the master returned for his filthy cloth. Smirking, he'd draw it on once more.

Foolish camels. *Never* would my revenge be attained by merely sullying the robes of a master. *Never* would my revenge be so spineless.

Perhaps this was not quite the moment for it though. The men-beasts replaced the daily stones with a hard saddle of wood and rug; next, they added panniers to hold weights more comfortably. It became a matter of amusement to learn the extent of my own strength.

Completing my training at last, I ferried old women and rich children—all foreign travelers—through the dry hills to the Valley of the Kings, the Ancient Ones. These burial places were hidden deep within rocky cliffs, but I learned about them as I listened to the talk around me. They held pictures painted on walls—and sometimes opulent treasures too.

Most rich children I did not mind. They cosseted me, feeding me treats of roots and sugar. They were not like the little beggar-beasts who followed us everywhere with their eternal cries of "*Baksheesh! Baksheesh! Spare a few coins, for the love of Allah!*"

In truth, it was not a hard life. I grew, always staring longingly into the real desert that called to me beyond the tombs—the desert that went on forever in the freedom of the burning sands. Soon I would break away again. This time I would be so strong and swift that no man-beast could follow me.

One day this all changed. The master—a dark and cheap man with a great, scruffy mustache—came to curry me. As he seldom performed this service, I knew something unusual was about to happen.

"Ah, my sleek Ali," he murmured. "You grow large. It is time to send you down the Nile. My brother awaits you in Cairo and will see to the rest of your training."

At this news I feigned a motion toward his currying hand. He swiftly pulled it out of range of my teeth.

"Heed me well, Ali"—one finger admonished me—"Abdullah is not a mild man like myself. Bite his hand, and you will know his fury!"

Exiled

Humph, I thought and spat a final time in the master's face. I had not submitted to this one . . . merely accepted a little training. It was highly unlikely that I would submit to his brother Abdullah.

I was attached to a caravan, and slowly we journeyed north on well-worn paths along the Nile to the man-beast Abdullah. After some days I began to see new sights. We passed other temples of the Ancients and finally drew near the greatest of their works: the colossal pyramids that rose up to pierce the sky. Even I was impressed. I paused at the view and spat reflectively. Mother had seen these as well. She would be pleased her Ali had come this far.

Then I met Abdullah. It was fortunate for both of us that our relationship was not destined to be a long one. This man-beast had a foul temper and a tremendous nose.

In the days following, I made every effort to relieve him of the latter, as I became rapidly convinced that here was one man-beast who did not deserve to breathe. Also, it was easier to nip at his nose than his ever-moving hands. Regrettably those hands usually carried a whip. I had never felt a whip before. Feeling it once was more than enough.

Abdullah took me and a few other camels to the true desert beyond the pyramids. There he mounted riders upon our backs and tried to train us to race.

I knew I was very fast. However, having taken an instant dislike to Abdullah, I had no desire to please him. Thus I ran very slowly.

Yes, there were moments when I was tempted to let go as I had at the camel market, moments when I wished to run for the sheer joy of running. But my stubbornness was stronger than my need to run. I feinted.

I balked. I yanked short in midstride and tossed my rider onto the burning sands.

Pah.

I would not submit to Abdullah's will. The angrier Abdullah became, the more I laughed to myself. This man-beast would never have his way with me.

Abdullah cracked first, but not without breaking a few whips upon my flanks. After a day during which I had been particularly belligerent, he let forth a stream of insults that would be abusive to anyone, no less to a camel who considered himself the ultimate in the wisdom of Allah's creation.

"Filthy creature! Witless son of a goat . . ." He ran out of taunts at last. "It is enough! What my brother saw in you I will never understand, but you will defy me not another day!"

His curses spent, he sought a suitable punishment for my behavior. At last he found it, and laughed uproariously as he led me into the city of Cairo, pausing in his mirth only long enough to inform me of his plan.

"I shall have my revenge upon you, Ali, many times over. And you know how I shall accomplish this end?" He grinned wickedly, his stained and broken teeth showing all the way to his gums. "It is perfect. Oh, so perfect! I shall sell you to the Christians! Let the Infidels be mocked by you to eternity!"

This brought me up short. *Infidels*? It was not a nice word. Yet had not the rich children who'd ridden on me to the Valley of the Kings been called that behind their backs? And had they not fed me roots and sugar? Could Infidels be worse than Abdullah?

Abdullah gave me a kick, and I continued walking, more curious than resigned. My fate was in the hands of Allah.

Exiled

◆ ◆ ◆

The Cairo bazaar wound in labyrinthine paths around a huge, domed mosque. Everywhere were tiny shops, everywhere the bedlam of voices hawking wares: rugs, copper pots, cloth, rare spices, and incense. Everywhere were buyers haggling for the best price. The aroma of mint tea wafted past my nose, enfolding it all.

To these sounds and scents was added the cry of the muezzin singing his call for prayer from the minaret outlined against the sky:

Allah is most great. Allah is most great. . . .
I testify there is no God but Allah. . . .
I surrender to Allah. . . .

Abdullah jerked me to a stop while he faced Mecca and knelt for midday prayers. I lowered my forelegs and bowed my head as my mother had taught me. Too soon this moment of respite passed. I was yanked up again to face a true Infidel.

He did not look evil. He was tall and pale—except for dark strokes of elaborately arranged face hair he wore for decoration. And his blue uniform was handsome. Abdullah called him "Major-Sir."

"Major-Sir!" Abdullah shouted for the man's attention. "Major-Sir! You seek camels for your great country. I have here a camel worthy of your notice."

Abdullah continued to speak loudly, bowing and scraping all the while. Is this how one treated a despised Infidel?

"What's wrong with him?" snapped the officer.

"Wrong? Major-Sir. Never will you find another camel as fine as this! I swear on my mother! Look at his teeth—he is young. Look at his flanks—"

"I'm looking. Why have you whipped him?"

"Major-Sir." Abdullah shrugged. "A camel must learn who is his master, must he not?"

As I'd never considered Abdullah my master, I lunged toward his nose with bared teeth. The results were gratifying. Abdullah leaped back, covering his scarred beak protectively. Major-Sir chuckled.

"I like a creature with spirit, that I do. What do you want for him?"

I didn't condescend to follow the bargaining. Instead, I examined the string of camels Major-Sir had already purchased. They were not much older than I, and none of them had the sickly look a city camel takes on. Also, there was a particularly comely female among them. I glanced back at Major-Sir with new interest. Perhaps he had a good eye for our race after all.

When the business was concluded, Abdullah shoved Major-Sir's money inside his robes and began to back away.

"One moment!"

Abdullah sidled back, rubbing his hands. "Major-Sir? I can be of additional service?"

"What is this camel's name?"

"You may name him anything you like, Major-Sir, but when he has not been called the devil himself, he is known as *Ali*."

"Thank you."

I looked upon Major-Sir with further regard and shot a nice wad at his feet.

Major-Sir roared with laughter. The sound rumbled from deep within his chest, like a camel. "Come along, Ali. We're off to the port of Alexandria, and from there across the ocean. You're going to have thousands of miles of American desert to spit in."

Three

I first met Hadji Ali in Alexandria on the docks near the ship that would take us on our sea voyage. Very small and lean of flanks, he was wandering around with a hungry look in his eyes. I noticed him observe Major-Sir struggling with some of the other camels, trying to convince them to leave the land for the large vessel before us.

Maybe it was because we had the same name that I responded as I did. Perhaps it was because he came to me and fearlessly patted my nose before I could even contemplate biting him. Although I still considered any man-beast beneath me, Hadji Ali was the first to whom I deigned to offer a measure of respect. Major-Sir noticed.

"You, there!"

"It is to me you speak, Effendi?"

Major-Sir tossed the harness he was holding to an underling. "Yes, please. Do you know camels?"

"I have looked upon them all my life, Effendi."

"But can you handle them? I'm in sore need of a camel master—"

"For food, Effendi? And pay?"

"Certainly for pay. Good United States currency as an employee of the army. Of course, you would have to travel to America with us—"

"When, Effendi?"

"As you can see, we are embarking at this moment."

Exiled

Our new master of camels bowed. "I am Hadji Ali, at your service, Effendi."

Major-Sir actually stuck out his hand and grasped the other's. "Splendid, Mr. Hi-Jolly. Help us load the animals, and then I'll take you to the mess for a good feed."

Hi-Jolly—for so he was to remain forever after—rubbed at the bony ribs beneath his *gallibiya* and smiled. I nudged a companion and laughed. Here was a man-beast almost worthy of a camel. Because of hunger, kindness, and native wit, he had been put in charge. There might be some hope for understanding between us.

Led by Hi-Jolly, I mounted the gangplank of the ship. Once aboard I paused for a moment before being lowered belowdecks. I knew neither where nor how far this America was. Yet I sensed it was a voyage of no return. The Mother of All Rivers was behind me, the open sea ahead.

I gazed back over the land of my birth a final time to admire the sky split by minarets, to smell the smells of a hot, dry land: the perfume of dates and open sewers and unwashed humans. It was all I had ever known.

Allah be with me. And you, too, O my mother, wherever you are.

Perhaps Hi-Jolly was saying his own good-byes. He allowed me my moment, then gave me a gentle nudge with his hand. I yielded to my destiny.

Belowdecks, the ship had been made into a huge khan. I received a stall of my own. A large white bull was stabled to one side and on the other was the fair, tawny female I had noticed in Cairo. I spoke to the female first.

"I am Ali, O Flower of the Desert. What is your name?"

She turned her head from me shyly. The name, when it came, was spoken softly.

Exiled

"Fatinah."

"Fatinah." I was charmed. The name of this loveliest of creatures meant "fascinating," "captivating," "enchanting." And it was so. All other she-camels in the world paled before this Fatinah. I almost spoke my thoughts aloud, before the bull on my other side intervened.

"Fatinah has not yet chosen a favorite. She is not of age. Neither are you, though your golden tongue belies the fact."

I bristled and lunged my head to try for a proper nip at this interloper's neck.

My neighbor merely sniffed. "Hold your temper. I, Seid, will deal with both of you when we are upon proper land once more. Until then, let us try to remain civil."

I turned my head from Seid and searched for something to eat as a face-saving measure. Alas, I found only a pile of hay such as donkeys graze upon. I nosed the fodder with disgust, then vented my ire upon it.

"What is this rubbish the Infidels feed us? Do they not understand the stomachs of a camel?"

"It smells very fresh and pleasant, Ali," whispered Fatinah. "Do try it."

I kicked my stall in answer. "They'll not make a donkey out of me! My mother did not raise me so!"

Just then Hi-Jolly appeared, rubbing a stomach that seemed considerably fatter than the last time I had seen it. He stood in the aisle like a favorite uncle, beaming upon the facing rows of camels.

"Ah, my impatient ones, do not fuss so. Do you not know that these American Infidels are richer than pashas? We go to a land of milk and honey, my friends. And we go together. Here now." He made straight for my stall and pulled something from beneath his robes. "For you, Ali, who brought me a future . . . for you I have something special."

I stopped kicking and nosed the treat from his hand. It was one of those sweet, orange roots. I chewed it with pleasure.

"You see?" Hi-Jolly murmured in my ear. "Sweeter than the juice of pomegranates. More pleasant than a cool sorbet after the heat of the day. Our fortunes will be as fine."

I snorted as the ship began to lurch.

We were on our way, bound for America.

It was a long voyage. Although my comrades and I could never see the waves of the sea, we felt them. Although we could not assess our progress, Hi-Jolly informed us of it with regularity. He spoke as he filled our water troughs, swept our stalls, groomed us, forked out more of that unending donkey food.

It was "Today we pass Malta," or "The coast of Spain is upon us," or "The Pillars of Hercules himself open before us!" And then it was "The sea. There is nothing but green and gray waves wherever the eyes alight. The sailors claim it goes on forever."

I studied Hi-Jolly more carefully. Truly he seemed to have taken on the hue of those green waves of which he spoke. The lantern light was not strong, but still one could see he was not feeling his best. For myself, the rough movements of the great ship were hardly discomforting. Was I not a kind of ship myself? A Ship of the Desert? A being who could stand the constant swaying back and forth across mountains of sand—mountains whose footholds could be as treacherous as the waves of a bottomless sea?

Hi-Jolly, however, was only a man. And yet . . . the fatness that had grown upon his bones while we sailed across the calmer waters before the Pillars of Hercules slowly melted from him. It melted like the hump of a camel at the conclusion of a long caravan with too few oases. I considered this curious state. His groans also offered food for thought. Beyond doubt he could groan like the best of us, green as he was. Could Hi-Jolly be part camel himself?

"A week already upon this wretched Atlantic," he moaned one day. "And no end in sight. By Allah, should we ever set foot upon the solid earth once more, I swear I shall avoid water for the rest of my natural life!"

Confined as I was within my stall, it was necessary to find what amusement I could. Fatinah was still shy, so out of necessity it was to Seid that I turned. Seid was perhaps a year or two older than I and nearing his maturity. Thus he had seen more than I. As we spoke during the long days and nights, I found a grudging interest in his words. Seid had been on a true caravan: across the Sinai, across Arabia, to Baghdad and back again.

"It was not easy, Ali, I can tell you. Five hundred pounds upon my back, day in and day out—often night in and night out, in the season of heat. Fifteen miles a day. Twenty miles a day. The sands burning my footpads, the storms sending biting bits to flay my skin. It made me wonder how our ancestors could have chosen such a route."

"What do you mean, *chosen*?"

Seid snorted. "It is easy to tell you have never ventured so far. All great caravan routes were first made by *us*, then stolen by the men-beasts."

"How could that be?"

But Seid was far away again, recalling his trials.

"A thousand of us were in that caravan. To the front, an unending column of camels. To the rear, the same. And only rarely the respite of an oasis, or a caravansary where we could rest for a night within the sheltering walls of a courtyard while our masters slept."

"Did you see strange sights?"

Seid's eyes came back into focus. "What kind of sights?"

I didn't have to think for long. "Monuments of the Ancients? Signs of Allah? Surely our kind would have picked such a way from the beginning."

Seid spat. "I saw nothing but rock and sand. I learned to march over both to the songs of the masters. The songs, at least, helped."

His words bewildered me. I had always thought there was more waiting out there in the world. Wonders to be learned. My mother claimed there were new wonders wherever one chose to look.

"What of your milk days?" I tried again. "And your mother?"

Seid spat again, more vigorously. "Of

them I had none. I was raised from a goatskin."

This brought a soft sigh of pity from Fatinah on my other side. So. She had been listening too. Seid was an orphan. It explained much—of what he had seen and what he'd left unsaid. It also meant he must be watched. He would have had no softness from a mother and would play upon Fatinah's gentle nature.

There were others to meet. At the far end of the hold, so far that I could just catch a glimpse of him, was a stranger among us—a two-humped camel. Of him I learned little save for his name, Hamid. Of all the camels, Hamid the Bactrian was the only one who became sick and stayed sick for the length of the journey.

The remainder of us were Arabians and dromedaries of a dozen different breeds, which created havoc on particularly long days.

Some camels would thrust their necks beyond the ropes that enclosed us. They expected admiration, of course—of their graceful lines, of the boldness of their neck brands, of their delicate coloring. Of just anything.

Next, they would move on to recite their genealogies till I could barely bite back my true feelings for such wanton display. After all, I was *Mahazi* of *Bechaniah*—the best, as my mother had assured me. But did I boast of that? And Fatinah was *Nomanieh,* bred to a different gait, but equally fine. Only Seid was unsure of his lineage, and I felt it in poor taste to throw this lack of knowledge in his face. Secretly I believed that with his natural self-esteem and fine carriage, his breeding was not deficient. The only quality missing was a care for others—something a mother would have taught him.

The boasting continued. Everyone knew racers were superior to load carriers. But those wrestlers! We had the ill luck to be burdened with no less than a quartet of them. Their conceit was enough to churn all four of one's stomachs at once. And Omar was the worst.

"I am *Omar,*" he bellowed constantly, "a true *lok* from Smyrna. My old master kept more than a score of us for the amusement of his wife, who loved watching our bouts. Wrestling is the finest of all sports: learning to throw your opponent, bringing him to the ground with just the right amount of body weight—"

"Why are you here, then, mighty wrestler," Seid interrupted, "if your value is so high?"

Omar glared down the aisle at Seid. "My mistress died, and the master had no further taste for us. But the wrestling art is not lost.

My fellow Pehlevans and I will take on any of you when we reach dry land. Especially *you,* Seid."

"Omar speaks truly," the other three always added. Then they would cast wicked glances around the hold of the ship, just waiting for a challenge. There were none then. But my temper was sorely tried, and I could tell from the grinding of his teeth that Seid felt the same. We would bide our time till our arrival.

Many days into the journey there was a storm. It was most ferocious in nature. Even I could not compare it to the desert. The ship heeled more times than I care to remember. Great numbers of men-beasts came—even Major-Sir and a doctor—to strap us tightly to the decks. Still we were jostled and banged and bruised . . . and then the water arrived. It poured into the hold of the ship until even I could see its color. But it was neither green nor gray. It was *black* and *cold* as it crept around our folded legs. Hi-Jolly followed it, lurching and frightened.

"Allah have mercy! Save us from the perils of the sea!"

I watched as he assumed a praying position in the gathering waters. But it was not a prescribed praying time. He had fallen. Hi-Jolly's head popped out of the brine.

Wet and furious, he spluttered, "Curses on this ocean! May every creature beneath it have eternal unhappiness! May they have the camel's itch—"

Argh. Hi-Jolly's words caused me to shudder from more than the chill waters. *Nothing* was worse than the camel's itch. Praise Allah, I had never been afflicted with it. But I had seen camels in Abdullah's keeping whose skin was coated with hot tar for the cure. Others he'd forced to swallow vats of boiling, vile concoctions. . . .

Aiyeeeeee!

A high-pitched shriek halted my unwanted memories—and Hi-Jolly's curses. Even the storm seemed to stop for an instant as the shriek sounded again, frantic with pain. From whence did it come?

Aiyeeeeee!

Again. It came from across the khan. I stretched my neck between the ropes as best I could. The cry burst from a female I'd paid little attention to as she had no given name, being called only by number. Hi-Jolly pushed himself up and staggered to her side.

"What is it, my pretty? What has hurt you?"

The problem soon became apparent even to me. The female was about to give birth in the very midst of the tempest!

"Ho! Major-Sir! Ho! Doctor Ray!" Hi-Jolly bellowed for help, all the while trying to undo the leg straps of Number Nine. Fatinah averted her gaze from what followed, while I unsuccessfully tried doing the same.

It was a difficult birthing, made more so by its unexpectedness and the convulsions of the sea. Major-Sir and the doctor assisted Hi-Jolly through the night. At dawn, as the storm eased, there was a new member of our corps. The cow was exhausted, but the men-beasts were quite pleased with themselves.

"He's really a handsome little fellow, Major Wayne," the doctor proclaimed. "What shall we call him?"

Major-Sir smiled as he helped Hi-Jolly guide the babe toward his mother's milk. "As we are on Uncle Sam's business, I believe he would be honored with a namesake."

I was never sure who this Uncle Sam was, but the young one took his name from that moment onward. He became a favorite of all of us, and one of the few bright spots during the remainder of the voyage.

As soon as Uncle Sam was old enough, Hi-Jolly exercised him every day. The rest of us rarely left our stalls, but this little one walked freely by Hi-Jolly's side while the cameleer dispensed treats of crushed pease or barley dough balls. As the youngster grew, some of the rough sailors began coming down to our khan to teach Uncle Sam how to wrestle.

The Pehlevans did not approve of the methods being used.

"Most unorthodox," spat Omar. "These Infidels know nothing of the traditions of true camel battle. Look how they instruct that calf! The neck, Uncle Sam! And the teeth! With the neck and teeth you can destroy!"

"Feint more to the left!" yelled another of the wrestlers.

Uncle Sam ignored his elders. He was under the misapprehension that Hi-Jolly was his father and these Infidels his playthings. Still, he learned something. And Seid and I chuckled to see his progress, orthodox or not. Perhaps the sailors felt differently about this after awhile—especially when at six weeks of age Uncle Sam flattened one of the men-beasts with his powerful forelegs, then went on to bash him playfully with his neck and mouth. Finally he stopped and grinned up at the rest of us.

"See how I've beaten these sailor-beasts at their own game?" he asked. "You bet they'll be more careful from now on!"

Ah, I thought. The calf was learning that he was a camel after all.

"Take care yourself, young one," growled Seid, "lest their tempers overcome their good humor."

Uncle Sam and the wrestling were a much-needed diversion from our boredom. Would the end of the voyage never come to pass?

Four

"America! She appears! The American Texas! We are saved!"

We arrived within view of the land at last. It was the Year of the Infidels 1856, in the moon they called May. Hi-Jolly rushed through the khan toward me, flung his arms around my neck, and gave my nose a big kiss!

"Oh, Ali, Ali. Three months of my life spent upon this wretched water!"

Still he clung to me. I regurgitated a big lump of donkey hay from my nearest stomach and made ready to bestow it upon him, then thought better of the gesture and swallowed it again. He never noticed.

"You shall be the first, Ali. The first to leave the *U.S.S. Supply*!"

"*Humph,*" I muttered. "We shall see."

It took two more days till the seas slowed enough for us to leave the ship. Then, indeed, I was given the honor of being the first to disembark. It was a dubious honor at best.

A sling was strapped around my middle, and I was hauled from the hold to the outer deck of the ship. There I shut my lashes tightly against the long forgotten light of the sun.

When I opened my eyes at last, I stood beneath sails that flapped like tremendous robes around sticks taller than minarets. There was no time for admiration. I was hooked to another, greater sling. Amid the groanings of many sailor-beasts, my noble weight was hoisted into the very air above the ship. . . .

And there I stayed.

And swayed.

Back and forth. Back and forth.

Both Major-Sir and the doctor were below me, as were many others I had never laid eyes on during the entire voyage.

"Higher!" Major-Sir shouted as he pointed toward a smaller vessel bobbing alongside. "More to the left. The left, you dolts! Now ease up. Ease up!"

"The winch!" a sailor-beast cried. "It's frozen!"

I was left swinging. Yes, swinging, while all below me swarmed around the broken device. I was neither of the ship, the waiting boat, nor the land so tempting in the near distance.

Humph.

My exile. My endless voyage. All had come to this degrading impasse. I bellowed my protests, to no avail. It was necessary to engage in combat.

My first wad was off target, but my aim improved. I spat fardels of green, half-chewed donkey hay that rained down on my tormentors. And still I swayed. When at last I bombarded Major-Sir himself, he relented.

"Enough!" He wiped the mess from his face. "The winch must be fixed—and the sea must calm itself. Release Ali."

I glared balefully at Hi-Jolly as he settled me into my stall belowdecks. He had the grace to apologize.

"I do not control the seas, Ali." He shrugged. "Or machinery. You know this too well. It was an honor I wished to grant you, after all. To be the first upon the new land."

His words flowed as he curried me,

wishing, no doubt, to obtain favor in my sight again.

"Still, your turn will come once more. We sail now for the mouth of a great river—as great as our Mother Nile, some say. There we will find quiet waters for the disembarking. This river, this Mississippi, should be our saving."

Careful not to let the others see, Hi-Jolly set down his brush to slip me the last of the root vegetables. It was withered and had lost much of its sweetness, but I accepted it in the spirit in which it was offered.

The Mississippi *was* calmer. It was wider than the Nile, and there were no monuments to the Ancients on its shores, no temples or pyramids. But then, we were allowed to see only a very small part of it while we were transferred to a smaller ship.

The second ship sailed some miles along the river to disgorge us upon the land at last.

"Hamdullah!"

Hi-Jolly threw himself prostrate on the shore, kissing the solidness beneath him. I lowered my forelegs to give Allah proper praise myself. Only then did I join in the joy of the other camels who were too frantic with excitement to remember to offer their Maker thanks for our deliverance.

Ayii. What a time that was! Harness and rope could not restrain us. Blessed heat and sun caressed our flanks as we frolicked on the good earth. Shipboard quarrels were forgotten, even by the wrestlers.

As my legs became steadier, I raced hither and yon between the land and the shore. I could have run forever. Finally I stopped to catch my breath. That's when I noticed Uncle Sam wobbling pitifully in circles, looking lost.

Fatinah and I met on either side of the young-ster.

"Why are you so bewildered?" I asked. "Are you not filled with delight at greeting the land?"

Poor little Uncle Sam began to bawl. "I don't like it! It's too still! I want my ship back again!"

I laughed, but Fatinah's look stopped me.

"Here now, small one," she comforted. "Watch your mother dancing over yonder. Does that not tell you that the land is good?"

Uncle Sam's shrieks slowed to hiccups, until finally he was composed. "Will I be able to walk whenever I choose on this land?"

"Whenever, yes," answered Fatinah gently.

He glared at me, unconvinced. "And *wherever?*"

"*Wherever* depends upon our masters. It always does." But not *forever*, I added to myself. Not forever. I looked up. For the moment, *wherever* and *whenever* both seemed to be now. Hi-Jolly and the sailor-beasts were beginning to close in on us, fresh ropes in hand.

"Come. It is time to discover what this Texas-America is like. It is not inconceivable that it, too, may hold wonders."

We marched some miles across flat, empty land with no vistas. There was not a single dune or temple to catch the eye. At last we arrived at a place that Hi-Jolly called an army camp. Our cameleer roused us with songs and shouts so that we entered the compound in high spirits. In fact, we entered with so much spirit that we frightened half to death the waiting soldier-beasts—not to mention their horses and mules.

I swaggered through the gates with Seid and Omar on either side. As they spied the braying mules, they roared with laughter.

"They have never seen our kind. Oh, what fun we shall have with them!" Seid chortled. In agreement for once, Omar nodded, casting his glance around, methodically choosing a victim for his mischief.

Seid was quicker. He stepped nonchalantly toward the nearest mule tethered to a wooden railing in front of a low, white building. First, the mule's eyes bulged. Next, he pulled his long ears flat against his head. Finally he leaped with more energy than all of us together had when we first reached the land. His cry of terror was heartrending.

"Have mercy upon the poor, simple creature," I growled to Seid. "Can you not see his heart is about to stop dead from palpitations?"

Seid feinted toward the mule, but did no more. A soldier-beast, sweating from the

61

heat—or fright—edged slowly toward Seid, making shooing motions. A second dragged the first by the scruff of his dirty woolen tunic out of range of Seid's teeth.

"Back off, Amos! Cain't you see that critter's got murder in his devilish eyes?"

Hi-Jolly caught up and gave Seid's rear flanks a sharp clip.

"Enough, Seid. This is no way to make new friends in a strange land. Repent and work only righteous deeds, as Allah hath directed."

Seid snorted but followed as Hi-Jolly led us to our resting place.

All had been made ready for us. Our quarters in a large khan were roomy. We had fresh bedding and access to a nicely parched field. Once our restraints were removed, though, my brethren and I ignored the mangers of donkey hay within and raced to the barrier at the far edge of the field.

Could it be? Yes! Joy of joys, it was a vast hedge of thorn brush!

Within minutes every camel except young Uncle Sam was munching ecstatically on this living fence. I glanced up from my feast long enough to notice Major-Sir standing nearby. He shielded his eyes from the setting sun, the better to study us. Then he began gesturing wildly at the master of the new place.

"Commandant!" he shouted. "Sir! Did no one take the time to read the directives I sent ahead? These animals will eat through that thorn and free themselves in no time! They must be stopped!"

The commandant was dubious.

"Nonsense, Major Wayne. It's not possible. We're short on wood here. Everybody uses thorn or prickly pear for fencing."

"Can't you see what's happening with your own eyes?"

"There's no animal dumb enough or tough enough to digest that thorn, Wayne."

"Nevertheless, my camels are doing it."

Beside me, Omar ripped a huge clump from the barrier. The commandant removed his hat to scratch his head thoughtfully.

"Perhaps you have a point . . ."

I turned my own head back to the hedge. Major-Sir always had his way in the long run. Best to enjoy my first decent meal in moons before it was torn from me.

This Texas-America was different in little ways. Consider the jackrabbits that bounded from holes all over one's grazing area. The soldier-beasts were fond of using them for target practice: jackrabbits and sinuous, slithery creatures called rattlesnakes. These rattlesnakes were much larger than the asps that had destroyed Cleopatra in my homeland—and even more lethal. Still, one had to be more on guard from the soldiers' poor aim.

Then there was the heat. It wasn't any hotter than on the banks of the Nile, but this was a damp heat I was unused to. It matted my hair and curled the tip of my tail. And the silly natives—they worked in their stifling blue tunics and heavy leg coverings instead of long, thin robes that would have cooled them. They were always forcing water on us, too, thinking we had the same needs as their horses or mules.

There were likenesses as well. These new men-beasts stank the same of sweat and dirt as our masters at home. Why then were they so surprised at our smell? Some of them would stand away, holding their noses in a most insulting manner. One morning as our doctor was examining us, a particularly sharp-beaked officer-beast asked him how he could stand the stench.

"Stench? Maybe I've been aboard ship with them too long. They smell natural to me."

"*Natural?* My dear Doctor, there may be heights to which the imagination cannot soar—just as there are depths to which I would prefer it not descend." He held a handkerchief delicately to his nostrils. "This is one of those depths."

"Get upwind of 'em then and stop complaining, Lieutenant. I'll not have 'em maligned in my hearing." And the good doctor proceeded with his examination of Hamid's footpads.

We stayed at that camp for some weeks since Major-Sir wanted us to do what he called "acclimating." Part of this acclimating involved our carrying load-bearing saddles. We marched with riders to the nearest town, where we were much admired. So much admired, in fact, that one day I overheard Major-Sir complain that he was fed up with the circus and was moving us to a new place. Soon Hi-Jolly was grooming us for the march.

"We go to Camp Verde, Ali, near to a place known as San Antonio. There is more grazing there. It will be good."

We moved out. It was a journey of several weeks, with layovers at army forts along the way for the benefit of our weaker members. I made believe that we were on caravan, going to the fabled lands of the East from my old country. But the daydream was spoiled by the wagon-pulling mules in the train who slowed us and the lack of the great dunes of sand rolling off into eternity.

As the novelty of this new place faded, I began to grow homesick. Neither the bells that jangled from my harness nor the songs of Hi-Jolly could comfort me. Not even the new, luscious treat of prickly pear cactus dotting our path was consolation enough.

One night, preparing for our evening's rest, Fatinah chose to lower her body next to mine. "You are troubled, Ali," she murmured softly. "Tell me of your sadness."

I grunted dismally as she gently nudged me with her soft mouth. "We will never again set foot upon our homeland, Fatinah. We are exiles forever, moving into the western sun when it is the East my heart longs for."

Fatinah chewed her cud, carefully considering. "That is so. You are not the only one who has had this thought."

"What must I do?"

"You survived losing your mother, Ali, as did I. We will survive this too. But you must eat. We must be healthy and strong to make this new land ours."

I flicked my lashes and listened to her

more carefully. "You are willing to do this?"

"We have no choice, Ali. You saw the ship leave. It will not return for us. And I myself would not wish to endure that voyage yet again."

"Then I must resign myself to this Texas-America?"

"It is very large. Perhaps there is more than what we have seen already. But do not resign. Accept. It is better, and it gives one a future."

"A future?" I looked at her with more interest.

"Yes, Ali, a future. Now we are friends, but someday . . ."

My heart began to beat very fast. If there was a chance that Fatinah and I . . . the land would not seem so alien.

"Fatinah—"

But Seid chose this moment to approach. He settled himself facing both of us. "Pleasant enough evening for this Texas-America," he drawled. "No sandstorms. Have you noticed that, Ali? I have smelled not a single sandstorm since we arrived in this land. I could not bear them."

My heartbeat slowed. So much for my intimate conversation with Fatinah.

Yet Fatinah's words stayed with me, and grew. The next day as we marched through a tiny village, I strayed to consume a high hedge of prickly pear next to the mud walls of a hut. The tubers of the cactus were particularly plump and fleshy as I bit through the spines to the moist center. The hut's owner, an old woman who'd been peering suspiciously through an open window as we passed, ran screaming out her door.

She wore no veil as did women of my homeland. Her screech came out more loudly without it, and her face was frightening to behold. Wispy gray hair flew and eyes burned with rage.

"Scat! Beat it, you heathen varmint! That's my garden wall you're eatin'! *Shoo!*"

I took a final bite as Hi-Jolly calmly ambled up and nudged me from harm's way. He was grinning. "Very content I am to find you eating again, my Ali; but we must choose our food with discretion, as with all things. Save your appetite for outside the village, eh?"

Other natives had crowded around to stare, among them a young woman akin to a goddess on a temple wall. She was unveiled also, but in her case mercifully so. Hi-Jolly did not miss the sight. His grin broadened. "There are definite compensations to this country, Ali. As soon as we settle ourselves, I intend to pursue them."

Five

"Ali, Ali . . ."

Hi-Jolly was not pleased by Camp Verde, and I was the ear for his complaints.

"We are so far from everything, Ali! Only look about you. Where are the cities? Where are the lovely ladies? Where, oh, where is civilization?"

I looked. Indeed, the temptations of the camp were few for such as my cameleer, especially since we were to remain there almost a full cycle of moons: through the cool and the cold and the warm again. Yet for a camel the expanse of arid land was not unwelcoming. Our grazing area was large. The khan Major-Sir had constructed for us was also large and airy—built like the ones in my native land, but cleaner. Hi-Jolly's quarters were cobbled onto the rear of our stable like a wart upon a huge nose, so he was always near.

To Hi-Jolly's relief, we did make small expeditions into the city of San Antonio. This was the largest place of habitation I had seen since our arrival, but it was as a gnat next to an elephant in comparison to Cairo. And there were no minarets, no muezzins calling the faithful to prayer.

Instead, there were church bells. The smell of mint tea was replaced by the tangy odor of dried peppers, which hung everywhere. These were not suitable for consumption. I should know, having tried a bite from a string in the marketplace one morning.

O my mother! O Ancient Ones!

Heat welled up in my head until I thought it might explode. I bolted frantically for the nearest horse trough and drank it dry. Still the burning in my throat remained—while my ears buzzed with derisive laughter from the soldier-beasts. My stomachs were not comfortable for two entire days.

It is not a memory I wish to retain. For moons thereafter I tempered my curiosity in matters of taste.

During this time, most of us were left to wander and graze as we wished. A handful of us were chosen, however, to take part in Major-Sir's experiment.

It was Omar and his friends who first got wind of the project. They'd been behaving themselves rather well, but signs of restlessness were beginning to appear. One day as I grazed peaceably in the middle of an empty range, ruminating over ancient mysteries, I was jarred from my meditations by a rough bump from a wrestler.

"Wake up, Ali!"

"Omar?" I blinked and retreated—not fast enough—as his neck swung toward me again. Even a playful bash from his kind could be painful.

"There are hectares of space out here, Wrestler." I shook the wool from my head. "Find some of it for yourself."

"*Acres,* Ali." Omar sneered, still blocking me. "Learn the new words for the new land."

"There is something wrong with the old ones?"

"Adjust with the land, Ali. It is progress."

My neck was sore when I tossed it. "I fail to understand what progress we have gained by moving from the old land to the new. Major-Sir has done nothing but parade us through town and allow us to grow fat."

"This will soon change, although I doubt you will join in the changes." Omar smirked, but he did relax the tension in his muscles. "You haven't the nature for *maneuvers.*"

I kept a few safe paces away from him. "What are *maneuvers?*"

"You see how much attention you pay to the important things around here? My fellow Pehlevans and I spy out the news, while you drift about, wishing for what's gone."

"What are *maneuvers?*" I was stubborn, if nothing else.

"Major-Sir will train us as a cavalry group. To bear riders and arms!"

"I already know how to bear riders."

Omar's chuckle turned derisive. "Not like the Zemboureks of Persia, you don't. I have seen this Dromedary Field Artillery on my travels." His eyes shone. "Oh, the colors of their harness, the brightness of the silken flags they bear! We shall be truly awe inspiring!"

"Thank you for the intelligence, Omar, but I have ideas to pursue." I bent for a mouthful of thorn. "I have almost resolved how a camel might pass through the eye of a needle."

Alas, Omar's howls of mockery completely destroyed the directions of my thought. After a sleepless night trying to grasp the lost threads of the solution, I was feisty enough in the morning to be hand-picked by Major-Sir for his artillery trials.

We began in the nearest horse corral. Uncle Sam, the she-camels, and the unchosen males gathered in clumps at the railing to watch. Hi-Jolly stood next to me, shaking his head at what he considered the folly of the experiment.

"Observe, Ali. Major-Sir calls the soldiers who will ride. Look how they line up for inspection. How tall they stand! Such shining brass buttons! These are the camp's best. But have they ever sat astride a camel? And will their shiny brass buttons help them? No." Hi-Jolly turned toward a mountain of metal cluttering a corner of the corral. "Cannons too. By Allah, does Major-Sir expect to shoot them from your backs?"

Major-Sir most certainly did. But first he had to train our new riders. The fancy soldier-beasts were soon sweat-stained, dusty, and out of humor. And when the great guns were slung across our humps along with these unseasoned passengers, few of us camels could rise from our knees. Blame the weight of the guns? No. We had the strength. Blame instead the clumsiness of the soldier-beasts. When would they learn that a camel's burdens must be balanced as delicately as the two sides of a scale?

Major-Sir stood ramrod straight in the midst of the corral, tugging at his face hair, watching men and guns topple around him. Oaths followed as freely.

Jenkins, my own rider, was especially determined. And mean. His horse crop smacked down upon my tender nose once too often. I struggled to my feet, took a full breath for balance, and swung my neck to give him a wallop worthy of the wrestlers.

"Son of a—"

Jenkins slid off my back and crumpled into the dust most satisfactorily. His heavy weapon landed on top of him. I could have added a few kicks to his body while he was down, but that seemed excessive. And anyway, Major-Sir was by my side in a moment.

"Ali, Ali. That was unfair. Still . . ." He bent to retrieve the offending crop. "Lieutenant Jenkins, I thought you told me you were studying the camels. More study and less crop, I should think."

Major-Sir strode off to the next disaster while the Jenkins-beast dusted himself off, gave me a grim glare, and tried again.

After a sweaty week of such antics, Major-Sir actually had our loads balanced. He'd made the camp blacksmiths add pivots to our wooden saddle pommels on which the guns could rest. Only then did he take the chance of opening the corral gates. He wanted to try the weapons away from camp.

We had not marched far when Major-Sir—weaponless and safely astride a horse—called a halt and pointed to a low bush in the distance.

"The enemy lies in wait *there,* men. It's a band of the most terrifying heathens, set on having your scalps. Take aim." He glanced over his troops appraisingly.

"Ready?"

"Yes, Sir!" barked the mounted soldier-beasts.

"Fire!"

The most terrifying heathens imaginable could not be worse than what erupted in an instant: a spine-numbing discharge from my back, earsplitting booms bursting through my ears, acrid smells of gunpowder billowing into my nostrils, Jenkins smashing into my hump. The combination was too much. I burst toward the enemy bush like the sword of Allah descending upon the wicked. My companions followed suit.

First Jenkins, then the weapon landed in the dust. And still I ran: past the demolished bush, past a rattlesnake once sheltered within it. My chest heaved, ready to burst. I snapped the very girths of my saddle and shed that too. Then I ran some more. Furlongs, miles. When I stopped, I was alone.

I had outdistanced everyone.

Ambling back to the khan that evening, I found Hi-Jolly waiting for me.

"So. I knew you would return, Ali."

I snorted a great *humph*. Of course! I could not run back across the seas.

"You will be pleased to hear that Major-Sir has discontinued his camel artillery experiment. He thinks perhaps its success might not be possible without a trip to Persia to observe the Zemboureks in action."

I pulled at Hi-Jolly's robes, hunting for a root.

He slapped my nose. "After what you did to that Jenkins today you expect the welcome of a prodigal son? The fatted calf?" Then he laughed. "If you could have seen the look on Jenkins's face, Ali! Not only did you leave him behind, you left that stinking

Infidel swallowing dust nose-to-nose with a rattler!"

Hi-Jolly roared. "Even so, he had only a twisted ankle and wrist. The snake was in worse condition. Now Jenkins will return with his crop to his fine horses. Let him beat them instead."

When I was settled in my stall, I glanced across the aisle to Omar. He and his wrestlers were the only ones who had wanted the honor of carrying artillery.

Omar bared his teeth at me and spat. "It could have worked. Major-Sir only forgot the colorful flags for our rumps. They would have given us pride. American Infidels have no understanding of the uses of pomp and circumstance."

With the moons of winter came an unfamiliar cold. But my coat was warm enough and the briskness of the air refreshing. Expecting nothing but the slow turning of time, I was surprised when Hi-Jolly woke me one morning, curry brush in hand.

"A special day this will be, Ali," he murmured. "We must ready all of you for new friends."

I stared at the cameleer without understanding.

"More camels, Ali!" he explained. "Another shipful that Captain Porter himself has brought!"

More camels? I wondered. When Major-Sir had found no use for those of us already here in Texas-America? I tossed my head at the folly, then decided to enjoy the grooming and the adornment in my best harness and jingling bells.

Outside the gates of the camp, we waited in expectation. I could smell my new comrades coming long before Hi-Jolly could see them. My old friends could too. Excitement began to build. Soon the caravan appeared, making its way across the flat landscape.

When the newcomers arrived—more than forty strong—we roared our greetings, but they returned them only halfheartedly. Perhaps the sea had been even more unkind to them than it had been to us. Hardly had they settled in than Major-Sir, who made it his business to visit us nearly every day, appeared. He inspected the new camels, walking through the khan as the day ended. He stopped at each stall, including those of us who were already veterans. Finally he reached mine.

"Good-bye, Ali." He patted my nose comfortably while I gave him a quizzical look. "I really do believe I shall miss all of you. But I've been reassigned, and I fear this is the last I shall see of you."

Major-Sir was leaving? A curious sorrow stirred in me over this man-beast's departure. He was, after all, one of the few remaining connections to my native land. It was he who had removed me from the clutches of Abdullah. It was he who had overseen my voyage and introduction to this Texas-America. I nudged at his hand for another pat, then felt foolish for being sentimental. I had sworn to my mother never to succumb to men-beasts, after all.

But had I actually submitted? No, I reflected. I had not. They, however, had required little of me thus far. Neither had I been badly mistreated by these Infidels. Never had I seen a camel along the banks of the Nile given such consideration. Why then did I still yearn for freedom? It was a hard question. I was still too young to know the answer.

As Major-Sir moved to the next stall, I roared across the broad aisle at Seid and Omar. "Major-Sir goes. Should we not bid this good master a fine farewell?"

Their answers were wicked grins, but the idea tickled them all the same. They in turn yelled to the two-humped Bactrian and the remainder of the wrestlers. The females joined in. Soon the whole khan was vibrating to the bellows of camels.

Major-Sir reached the door and paused for a moment, smiling.

"So it should be."

He swept off his hat and made a bow to us. "The grand endeavor of the United States Camel Corps is finished for me but is only beginning for you. Perhaps you will not succeed as an artillery unit, but the desert waits. Serve your masters and the brand new President Buchanan well, my friends. There is still greatness possible in your futures!"

Clapping his hat back upon his head, Major-Sir marched out of our world.

◆ ◆ ◆

I wondered how all this coming and going might change our lives. New camels, new masters who gave orders from the mysterious place called Washington City. While grooming me one morning, Hi-Jolly tried to explain about this President Buchanan whom Major-Sir had mentioned.

"Buchanan arrives with something called an *election,* Ali. It seems to be a curious ritual these American Infidels perform every four years to choose their new sultan. Such a luxury might occasionally be of use in Egypt, I can tell you. Still, this Sultan Buchanan and his new retainers might have other ideas about camels. We can only wait and see."

While I waited, I grew larger. I was content for the moment to be grazing peacefully near Fatinah and Seid, whom I had come to like in a grudging kind of way, even with his occasional roughness of spirit. When the heat of the summer returned, the change hinted at by Hi-Jolly came at last. It came with the arrival of a new Infidel master called Edward Beale.

As usual, it was Hi-Jolly who brought the news.

"Come, Ali." He appeared to collect me from the field. "The great Beale has arrived. He is a man of parts, a man who has done things. The soldiers whisper it was he who brought word of the Gold Rush to Washington City. Perhaps he knows of other secrets and riches. Riches that could be ours too, eh?"

Hi-Jolly pulled my halter impatiently, and I began to follow.

"He will choose twenty-five camels to make a caravan across the desert beyond Texas-America. You and I, we must be among the chosen, yes? The army needs a new road built through the desert to carry mail quickly and to supply its posts—"

I stopped. A new *road*? Here was *real* camel's work at last. I roared a tremendous roar of satisfaction. Hi-Jolly grinned.

"Together we will prove that camels can do this best. The road breaking and the transport too. It is why we were brought across the endless seas, is it not?"

I grunted and gave my neck a great shake. At last there would be purpose to my exile.

"I knew you would understand, Ali. We do not need any more time *acclimating* in this Camp Verde. It grows stifling here. It is time for some adventure."

He tugged at my rope, but halfway to the khan I dug in my hooves and turned.

"You have friends you wish to join us, Ali?" Hi-Jolly considered as I stared back to where I'd been grazing. He followed the direction with his eyes.

"Yes, Seid, of course. And perhaps Omar the wrestler? But what am I thinking? Fatinah must go too!"

I grunted my approval.

"Very well, Ali. I will make all of you magnificent. This Beale would be a madman not to choose you above the others."

Thus it happened that the next forenoon we were marched across the camp's parade ground. Beale stood at attention, appraising each of us. I held my neck higher and strutted more elegantly than I ever had. To make a road was important work, noble work, was it not? The great caravan routes of the East had been marked out by my forebears ages ago, and they still existed. Seid had marched across them, and so had Omar. Surely this was work that would have made even my father proud.

I uttered not a sound and stilled Seid

with a single glance when I saw that old wicked glint in his eyes. It was not the moment to spray this Beale with spit. Hi-Jolly halted us in turn to point out the lines of our flanks and to present our teeth for inspection.

"Open, Ali!" I opened my mouth.

"Kneel, Ali!" I knelt.

"Observe Ali's branded markings, Beale-Sir. He comes from noble lineage!"

I smiled with pride and tossed my neck. Beale had the intelligence to be impressed. I was chosen.

Then, eyelids half closed, basking in my acceptance, I heard a titter from the soldier-beasts surrounding Beale. Following their pointed fingers, I saw Uncle Sam. The young rascal was bounding across the parade ground like a Texas jackrabbit. There was a grin of youthful exuberance and expectation on his face. How had he escaped to follow us? No matter. He must not ruin our plans.

"What are you doing here?" I growled.

Poor Uncle Sam skidded to a stop. "I want to go with you! I want to see the rest of my country!"

"You're far too young," barked Omar. "Go back to your mother's teat."

"I am not too young! And my milk days ended moons ago!"

Hi-Jolly rushed up and grabbed Uncle Sam's harness. "Wicked child! You wish to embarrass me? You wish to show Beale-Sir I cannot control my camels?"

Uncle Sam gave a piteous cry. "But I don't want to be left behind!"

Beale was leaving the parade ground. Perhaps all was not lost. I walked toward Uncle Sam and Hi-Jolly. "Come now, little one, don't be so eager to leave your mother. Your chance will come."

"When?" Uncle Sam stamped his foot,

close to one of his tantrums. "And if it does, will it be as good as this one? And will my friend Hi-Jolly be with me?"

"I cannot answer those questions. Only Allah knows the future."

Caravan

And they carry your heavy loads
To lands that ye could not
[Otherwise] reach except with
Souls distressed: for your Lord
Is indeed Most Kind, Most Merciful.

XVI, 7
QUR'AN

Six

"A fine state of affairs. A fine state indeed!"

Beale was livid as he paced in front of us—his chosen pathfinders, his chosen camels. Uncle Sam was not the only one to be left behind. Hi-Jolly was too. So were the cameleers who'd come with the second ship.

"I tell you, Stacey, if the U.S. government cannot be relied upon to pay its employees . . ."

Stacey, Beale's assistant, kept a measured

distance from his master's wrath. "The Arabs claim they've seen no money since Major Wayne left in January, sir. You can hardly blame them for refusing to work a day more till they're paid the arrears. Still . . ."

"Still *what,* Stacey?"

Stacey studied us with trepidation. "How are we to pack the beasts, Mr. Beale, sir? We don't know *how!*"

Beale's wiry form stiffened. Like Hi-Jolly he was small, but passion and authority made him seem bigger. "You'll learn, Stacey. It can't be harder than surveying and constructing a new wagon road to California. We'll all learn."

If Allah did indeed know the future, I began to wish He had more of a sense of humor about it.

These impatient men-beasts did not learn easily. My comrades and I traveled to

San Antonio readily enough, as we were used to that route. Once we started blazing the new road, though, everything became harder. I almost forgot the greater purpose of the caravan, and I longed for dear, kind Hi-Jolly.

I was particularly upset by the actions of a certain soldier-beast in our party. Early in our journey he grew abusive to Fatinah. First, he placed her packsaddle awkwardly. Next, he proceeded to pile goods upon her back so haphazardly that any fool could see they would soon slip off. Her hump—how tender only a camel knew—was already aching. Consider the pain after a full day's march! Though she was the most patient of females, Fatinah complained.

The soldier-beast replied to her cries with the most vulgar of curses. Such words were unsuitable for her maidenly ears, and Fatinah protested more strongly.

How did this Satan among men-beasts respond? By violently kicking Fatinah in the softness of her belly. *No one* kicks a she-camel in this place, not even in my native land.

Laden with my own ill-packed burdens, I raced to her defense. Too late. My Flower lunged out—

"Aaarrrrgh!"

—and stripped the skin from the villain's forearm like thorns from a bush.

In the great confusion that followed, did any man-beast think to comfort my poor Fatinah? Never. Everyone's attention was focused on the screeching brute who'd brought his fate upon himself. Fatinah was abandoned—mortified that she'd had to resort to such a ploy for her self-preservation.

Humph.

No master could be trusted. How was it

that we, so much stronger than they, could not rebel and become our own masters?

Rebellion filled my mind as we trod on day after day, the burdens on our backs ever increasing at the whim of our masters. We no longer lost our loads every half mile along the way. The soldiers had become more adept at packing. But the loads had become much heavier.

The men-beasts took great pleasure in measuring what we carried. One morning it would be, "Five hundred-fifty pounds on this critter, Billy." The next it would be, "Keep loading, Billy. Beale needs to figure how much camels can carry before we get to California. Yesterday's load didn't do no harm. And them mules pulled their wagons bctter, lighter like they were. Let's push it up to six-fifty today."

It got so that after a few weeks Beale's

men had Omar—our strongest—burdened with almost a thousand pounds. Omar was not pleased. He shared his displeasure with us one evening, as we rested in a great circle from the day's labors, our heads turned inward.

"These men-beasts know nothing but lies," Omar began. "Our mission was to make a road—not push our strength to the breaking point."

We all murmured our agreement. Omar continued.

"Should the Infidels place one extra straw, verily *one single extra straw,* on my back tomorrow, *they* will be carrying the load. And I atop them, too."

This interested Seid. "Would you dare, Omar? Only once have I seen a camel of burden wreak such revenge. I was on caravan then, too, with a new cameleer testing himself against us." He spat reflectively.

"Who won, Seid?" I asked.

"Pshaw, Ali. Grow up. When we wish, we can do anything."

This I knew, but I'd been loath to share my rebellious thoughts. "It is one thing to bite a master, to show an independent spirit, another to—"

"That master never needed to test himself against us again." Seid's lips curled in remembrance. "When our leader, Old Gussuf, finally had enough, he left the cameleer flatter than a loaf of fresh-baked pita."

Fatinah turned her head away. "It is too terrible. I wish my temper had not overcome me with that soldier-beast. My poor mother would die of shame were she to know."

"Ah," voiced Seid, "but she will never know, will she, Fatinah?"

Fatinah gave him a stern look. "Does

that justify my act in the eyes of Allah?"

"We left Allah behind in our native land too, Fatinah," Seid shot back.

"No! I cannot believe that, Seid. Allah still protects us, and we have obligations in return."

Seid growled. "You sound like a mullah, Fatinah, though I never heard of a female priest. We are in a new land. Forever. You and Ali must learn to put away the religious scruples of your childhood."

Seid's thoughts shocked and repelled me. Rebellion against men-beasts was one thing, but rebellion against Allah? "'Ye have indeed rejected Him, and soon will come the inevitable.' Beware of Allah's punishment, Seid."

In answer Seid shut his eyes and turned away. The desert night closed in.

The land across which we journeyed became

hard. Flat, green pastures gave way to dry, scrubby desert erupting with curious hill formations the Infidels called *buttes*. The earth turned to sand, rough pebbles, and sharp scree.

All took its toll on the mules and horses that accompanied us. Though they had iron shoes on their feet, they complained constantly of the cruel shards of rock and hard lava upon which my fellow camels and I trod unprotected and unscathed. And there was rarely enough water for their needs, although always enough for us. When we neared a water hole or stream, the poor creatures pulled at their traces till the very wagons behind them toppled into the water.

It was, indeed, a barren land. Yet it suited me. Besides the tangy thorn and the occasional delight of a prickly pear, new tastes presented themselves as we marched forward under a hot sun. The soldier-beasts teased us, pointing to the fresh varieties with glee.

"Go on, Ali. See what you think about that there hackberry."

At first I held back, remembering the hot peppers incident. But in the end curiosity always overcame me. I would taste and find it good.

Next, it would be, "Bet you critters cain't tear into that mesquite!"

But we could, and we did. The leaves were moist. The shrub's spines slipped past my tongue smoothly, and the pods crunched with the sweetness of nectar. The men-beasts stood with their mouths gaping, so the ever-present flies swarmed right in. Then came their furious jigs and slaps, and cries of "Dad blast it!"

After the soldier-beasts had mastered the packing, Beale set them to other tasks.

Quite often they stopped us to extract long, three-legged objects from the supplies on our backs. These they called *surveying* tools, and they placed them at a distance from each other, marking the lengths between. After shouting numbers back and forth, they sometimes changed the direction of our route.

Sometimes, too, Beale stopped the caravan and ordered us to be harnessed. He wanted to test our power against great boulders.

Fatinah had not the strength for such work, but Seid and I pulled with will. We were determined to perform better than the horses and mules—even though I often wondered why Beale did not make his road around the offending rocks, as was done in the sands of the East.

Soon Beale, growing restless with the journey, began something he called his "practical jokes." These usually concerned the soldier-beasts' fear of creatures they called *Indians*, or *Comanches*. Not that we'd seen any of these creatures. What were they, I wondered? Huge animals, greater than camels? From the fright their very names produced, they must be quite extraordinary.

One day Beale split the party. He sent half of us ahead to find a camp while the others remained behind to pull more boulders. Those of us in the advance group arrived at a suitable site and were unloaded. The soldier-beasts busied themselves making a fire and setting out and testing their bedrolls.

"Hain't nothin' here but blasted scree," complained one. Taking his bedroll, he moved a distance off. Slowly the others followed, leaving behind the small fire around which we camels gathered in our usual circle.

We'd barely settled under the stars

when Beale came roaring into the deserted camp astride his horse, firing his gun and yelling "*Injuns!* Let's get the rascals, boys!"

That woke us up. I struggled to my feet, staring into the blackness; but even my fine night sight could distinguish nothing out of the ordinary. Beale continued his cavorting till his mount got fed up and threw him.

By this time the men came straggling in from their new camp.

"Where's the Injuns?"

"Ain't a soul but us . . ."

Beale heaved his body and his dignity from the dirt and brushed himself down with a wince.

"It was a test! Where were the camp's guards?"

After growling at the bewildered and sleepy men, Beale wandered off behind our circle and was noisily sick for the remainder of the night.

As the camp settled again, Fatinah favored me with a look.

"Where are these Indians, Ali?"

"No Indians, Fatinah. Rest."

"But I heard him say—"

"It was a joke."

"How can a man-beast joke about something so frightening?"

"Men-beasts are strange beings."

Seven

I finally learned what an Indian was. It had been another very hot, dry day, and we camels had just been unloaded. Suddenly a small band of scraggly, half-naked, dark-skinned creatures with feathers sprouting from their hair wandered on their ponies into view. Their hands were held out, weaponless.

Tension spread throughout the camp. Beale calmed his men as he inspected the visitors.

"They want to talk. They're signaling

for peace. But get your rifles to hand—discreetly." He spun around to where one of his men was already cocking his weapon. "Blast it all, I said *discreetly,* Farneswell. You want to get us all killed?"

Farneswell shoved the gun behind his back as Beale went to welcome the callers. They never got off their ponies, but there was much waving of hands. At one point Beale yelled back for some rations of tobacco. We watched him hand out the twists, one to each of the visitors. After more hand gestures the ponies whirled and disappeared.

"Can you believe that!" Beale chuckled as he walked back for his tin plate of food. "Those Comanches wanted to trade for the camels! I had to tell them they were the personal property of the Great White Father in Washington—and he'd look unkindly upon my losing any of them."

Exiled

Laughter spread around the campfire, and the tenseness dissipated. My comrades and I moved off a fair distance from the main camp. The soldier-beasts had been complaining about our odor again. We settled into our circle under bluffs that had shaded the ground during the afternoon, making our lying place cooler.

Just before sleep came I chanced to glance up at the cliff towering over me and saw a curious sight: a very dark-skinned man-beast's face, beneath the feathers of a bird of prey. He appeared to be one of Beale's recent visitors. I wuffled in interest and the head disappeared, as if it had never been there.

Fatinah caught my expression.

"What is it, Ali?"

"I am unsure. Possibly another of Beale's jokes."

"Ah. I pray to Allah that this one is less

unsettling than the last."

We dozed off.

Some time later a faint noise pulled me back from a dream of the great Mother of All Rivers. It was a wonderful dream, because I was there beside the water again, grazing with my mother. I had just thought to ask her advice about my current dilemma in a strange land when the outside scufflings intruded again. I did not wish to leave my mother's side until she had given me her wise answer, so I fought the sounds. I only opened my eyes with reluctance as the Nile—and my mother—faded away.

Then I was awake with a vengeance. Fatinah was gone! I jumped to my feet, searching with my eyes. Everyone else was asleep. The entire universe under the stars seemed asleep. Nothing moved. Except . . . was something stirring to the south?

Choosing my steps with great care, I set

off to investigate. Fatinah did not wander at night. Someone or something had captured her while I had been luxuriating in dreams of home.

Anger spurred me forward. I spied moving figures at last, then began closing in on them, always keeping a safe distance until I could learn what dangers lurked ahead.

The miles passed in this fashion as the sky began to grow light with the coming dawn. The creature who had stolen my Fatinah took shape. He was the same Indian-beast I had seen on the bluff. The feathers on his head stood out as proof.

Ahead were more horses and another of the feathered ones. I trotted behind a protecting boulder and watched the Indians dance in glee around the roped Fatinah. At last they led her farther south. Scrawny as they were, these Indian-beasts were more

dangerous than the soldiers of Beale's caravan. My mission became clear.

I must rescue Fatinah.

With the final rising of the sun, I settled
behind a clump of mesquite on a slope
overlooking the Indian-beasts' home. Safely
hidden, I stared down onto a strange sight.
The camp was not enormous, like Cairo. It
wasn't organized like the mud-walled huts
of villages in Texas-America. Neither was it
filled with the splendor of monuments to
the Ancient Ones that peppered the banks
of the Nile. Yet it held fascination.

Cone-shaped dwellings painted with
many pictures—like my favorite hieroglyphs—dotted the plain. Dark-skinned
men, women, and child-beasts cavorted
around Fatinah. Mangy curs yapped and
jumped as excitedly as their masters.

Slowly the frenzy stilled. Fatinah was
led to a small corral and set loose. The

extraordinary beings resumed their activities. I rose and sought a better hiding place in the shadows to wait out the day. Nothing could be achieved while the sun shone. The Indian-beasts' numbers were too great. I pulled at a few thorns, letting the chewing calm me. I would wait and plan.

As the day passed from high noon into late afternoon, I learned more as I observed these Comanches. They appeared scrawny. In fact they were strong, short-legged creatures who rode their horses as if born to them. Both males and females alike wore their hair long, but only the men's heads sprouted feathers. Some of the men also wore decorations of great, long teeth around their necks. The males either rode their horses or lounged around. The females were busy every moment, fixing fires, stirring cooking pots, scraping at something set on frames like the weaving I had seen females do in villages we'd passed during our caravan. But even from my distance I could tell they were not weaving cloth. They were laboring over skin similar to my own.

The hides gave me pause. The cauldrons did too. Were these Indians benighted enough—or hungry enough—to kill and eat Fatinah? A chilling thought, even in the heat of the day.

The camp settled into sleep. But slowly . . . oh, so slowly. Indian-beasts lingered too long around fires, picking their teeth, gesturing toward the corral that held Fatinah. During the afternoon, they had presented her with a harness that glittered with color in the last rays of the sun. Was my Flower being readied for a ritual? I shivered. My dreaming days were over. I must act with haste.

Exiled

❖ ❖ ❖

A crescent moon blessed the night. It was a fine omen. Was not such a moon the symbol of my homeland? When the moon had traveled halfway across the sky, I left my hiding place, descended the hill, and picked my way across the trampled grasses to the corral.

"Fatinah!" I murmured.

Her head swung up; long lashes opened. "Ali? Is it you? Or am I dreaming?"

"Hush. It is I. Can you jump over this railing?"

"I am hobbled, Ali. It is not possible."

"Then I shall come for you." I backed up for a running start, then bounded over the flimsy barrier as if it weren't there. All was accomplished with barely the scuffle of a pebble against the dry ground.

"Fatinah." I paused to nuzzle her cheek. Then, using my teeth, I grasped the leather thongs on one of her rear legs. It took a long minute for me to bite through, another to separate her foot from the wooden stake. I looked up.

"*Now,* Fatinah. Now you must jump that fence and follow me back to camp. Quickly."

She hesitated. "Do we know these Indian-beasts are worse than our own masters? They have treated me most cordially today. Did you see the decoration they gave me? It is prettier than any I ever had!"

"Fatinah." I sighed. "The first time they become hungry, you will be in the pot. If you have looked upon them, you will know their hunger is not far off."

Still, she didn't move.

"I feel sorry for them. They spoke of being chased from their homeland in the north by soldier-beasts. They are exiled just like us, Ali."

"All the more reason for us to leave. They are hunters and thieves, Fatinah. They stole you!"

"Yes, but . . ."

My impatience was building as I glanced at the sky. The moon was falling lower, and soon dawn would come. With the dawn we would both be captive.

"Fatinah. Do you want to be rescued? To be with me?"

"Of course I want to be with you, Ali. But to go back to Beale and his hateful soldier-beasts?" She paused. "Could this be the time to try for the freedom you've been speaking of? The two of us, alone?"

I shook my head. "No. Not here. These Indian-beasts are clever and could sneak up on us again."

She opened her lips as if to protest, but I quickly continued. "We must also finish our road. A great road lasts almost forever,

Fatinah. Our great-grandchildren will travel the road, the route we are breaking. They will feel pride in the knowledge of its builders. Pride in talents brought to this land first by us."

Her eyes began to shine as I continued to paint my vision.

"When we get to the end of our caravan and our job—the place called California— it will be time. Beale speaks of great deserts with dunes of sand just as in our homeland. In this desert—this Mojave—*no* men-beasts live. It will be our refuge."

Fatinah nodded acceptance, then her brow wrinkled as the barrier of the fence loomed before her.

"I'm not sure I can make the jump, Ali."

"Then I will broach the railing for you. But when it is down, you must run like the wind. Do you understand, Fatinah?"

"Yes, Ali."

Argh. Why was she so passive? So submissive? Why couldn't she think to fight her way out as I would? . . . Yet if she were made so, I would be unnecessary.

"Get ready," I whispered.

I eyed the wooden posts. It would take the kind of neck lunge I'd seen Omar and the other Pehlevans perform. It must work the first time. There would be no second chance, for the noise would wake the sleeping camp.

Now.

I thrust forward, swinging my neck like a battering ram. The barrier sundered with a crack that cut through the night.

"Fatinah! Run!"

I jumped the lower post, pausing only to see if Fatinah was following. She was. But so were the Indian-beasts. That one sound had roused the Comanches like a shot from

Beale's gun. But this was no joke. Already the feathered ones were leaping upon their horses.

"Run, Fatinah! Like the wind!"

It was a hard run, but it did not tire me. I had not raced like this since my baby days at the camel market. It was joyous. It was wonderful. And Fatinah raced beside me. My pride in her fed my speed.

We ran west, then north. After a few miles the mounts of the Indian-beasts were frothing, but we were not even winded. As the sun rose, I stopped to look behind. The Indian-beasts had given up the chase.

Fatinah and I found Beale's new camp as the evening's cooking smells were filling the sky. We were greeted as heroes.

"Well, lookey here who's come back. Sir! Mr. Beale! Them runaway camels found us!"

Beale came over to inspect us. He admired Fatinah first. "Stacey. Billy. Look at this. Far from being runaways, I do believe these camels were stolen. See the beading on the female's harness? Comanche."

Gasps rose around us.

Beale made a move as if to remove Fatinah's decorations, but she jerked her head away. It was a very definite *no.*

"A badge of honor, eh? Well, perhaps so. You may keep the finery."

Stacey thought to pat me. "Nothing on Ali, sir. You don't suppose he rescued her, do you?"

Beale stared into my eyes, and I stared back.

"I've heard of stranger things."

He shrugged and turned to the soldier-beasts gathered around us. "Give them both a good grooming. And anything else they might need. Lighten their loads for the next few days, too. Who knows how far they've been?"

Beale pushed through the crowd but stopped for a final order.

"And triple up on the guard tonight!"

Eight

"Ali, my friend!"

A surprise waited for us in the place called El Paso. As our caravan meandered through the dusty streets of the town, a familiar head popped through the beaded door of a shop the soldier-beasts called a *cantina*.

Hi-Jolly?

Our progress halted completely as the cameleer lurched toward us, a huge grin disfiguring his face. He swayed before me, arms spread wide to embrace my neck. "I have come back to you! Are you not pleased?"

Humph. I grunted and spat.

He backed off. "So. You feel I deserted you. This I can understand. But a man must stand up for himself, even in the land of Infidels. Else he is not a man."

Hi-Jolly squared his narrow shoulders. "Someday maybe you will know this. We should be worth our labor, man and camel alike. Still, I am back, with good U.S. coins to spend." He slapped my side. "Six months' back wages, Ali. Approved by the great sultan himself in Washington City. There are entertainments on which to spend them too." He jingled the pouch below his robes with a smile. "And the promise of more work all the way to California."

"Cut the gab, Hi-Jol," yelled one of Beale's soldiers from the wagon just behind. "Reunions are on your own time. We got furlough comin' soon's we stable these animals."

Hi-Jolly gave Billy a sloppy salute. "The

señoritas have been waiting."

Wild whoops burst from the soldiers all the way to our stopping place. Hi-Jolly staggered along and immediately began removing my burdens as if he'd never abandoned me.

"What's this? A saddle sore? A thousand curses upon these unfeeling soldiers! But I will fix this quickly, Ali. Before we move again. It is not yet bad."

So Hi-Jolly walked among us once more. He chattered, consoled, and spread acrid greases upon our backs into the night. I forgave him.

We moved north along the Rio Grande, arriving at a larger town called Albuquerque. Here we rested for a number of days while Beale went about some mysterious business. After the first night we learned that Hi-Jolly had his own mysteries to attend. He supervised our care in a very slapdash manner, then disappeared on the trail of the soldier-beasts—all heading for this Albuquerque. And in the morning there would be much wailing and breast beating, at least from Hi-Jolly.

Our cameleer began appearing late for his duties, looking almost as green as those days upon the sea. When we grunted, he would clutch his head in pain.

"*Hush.* Hush, my beauties. The cantina last night, it did me less good than the one the night before."

I could not understand the cause of Hi-Jolly's illness—the head pains, the periods of dizziness—until one of the soldier-beasts came trailing after him on the third morning. He motioned to his own head, which also appeared painful.

"Dang near drank us all under the table last night, Hi-Jol." He slapped our cameleer on the back. Hi-Jolly cringed, but not in fright. "Never knew a furriner like you could swallow wine so fast. All that back pay must be burnin' a hole in your pocket. And you was doin' pretty good with them dice for a while there, too."

Wine! Gambling! Our Hi-Jolly? Did he not remember the words of Allah and his prophets? 'In them is great sin, and some profit . . . but the sin is greater than the profit.' I gave him a baleful glance and shunned him for the remainder of the day.

On the morrow Hi-Jolly did not appear at all. Beale, however, did. He dashed into camp in his usual manner, anxious to return to road building now that his business was completed. When he found most of the soldier-beasts gone, he had Seid and me saddled, since his favorite horse was weary. Mounting Seid, Beale directed his assistant, Stacey, to mount me. Thus we rode into Albuquerque in pursuit of the missing.

It took a good part of the day, as the sol-

dier-beasts were spread among many cantinas. The method never varied. Neither did
the results. Beale and Stacey dismounted to
search a place. Finding one of their own
within, they caused a shocking disturbance:
crashes, bangs, yelps of terror. At last a soldier-beast or two was tossed through the
doorway and over the boardwalk to stagger
back to camp.

But it was worse for Hi-Jolly. There was
so much noise emanating from the cantina
into which Beale disappeared that I edged
closer to the open door to study the room
beyond. I must say, I could not understand
the allure of the place. It smelled foully of
sour wine and tobacco. It was not even pleasant to look upon.

Several rickety tables were upright. Men-
beasts cushioned their heads on top of them
in sleep. But several other tables—and
chairs—flew through the air! As they settled

to the floor, I picked out the form of poor Hi-Jolly. Beale himself had cornered him with one of the chairs.

"Please, sir, please! I come," pleaded Hi-Jolly.

Our cameleer cowered most abjectly, showing none of the spirit he claimed to possess.

"It is a changed man you will be seeing!"

"Changed indeed!" roared Beale, striking Hi-Jolly about the head and shoulders with the chair. "I'll not have a drunken lout attend my animals!"

Hi-Jolly stumbled toward the door, Beale's kicks raining upon his rear flanks. I pulled my head from danger and stepped back into the street. Seid gave me one of his wicked grins.

"Beale certainly took care of that!"

"You approve? Hi-Jolly is nearly one of our own. And he is in a state of weakness.

Surely it is unfair to be attacked at such a moment."

"You didn't complain when Beale kicked his own soldier-beasts."

"They deserved it for beating us these past moons."

Seid spat into the dust of the street. "Beale's all right with me."

"You begin to sound like one of these Infidel Americans, Seid!"

Seid merely grinned another wicked grin and lowered himself so Beale could remount.

Seid became Beale's favorite, even over his horse. As we continued westward, Seid no longer had to move boulders or carry any burden heavier than our leader. He and Beale roamed the length of the caravan many times in the course of a day, only pausing to confer with the surveyors. Sometimes they disappeared over the horizon while Beale went scouting for better routes. In the evenings Seid retold his adventures. But he did it in a haughty manner that began to wear. Resentment built among us—particularly in Omar and the other wrestlers who carried the heaviest burdens.

"How Beale could choose one of such lowly birth eludes me," Omar complained one afternoon as we watched Seid loping gallantly down the line toward us. "We wrestlers would look much finer in his position of honor." He spat. "We were not schooled to carry burdens or strain our shoulders in harness like water buffalo at the plow!"

"Don't be jealous of Seid's good fortune, Omar," Fatinah called from behind me. "He had such sad milk days. I am pleased to see him happy for once."

"It is not happiness he displays, but arrogance." Keeping a steady eye on his approach, Omar casually but effectively shot a wad at

Seid's white flanks.

I watched Seid's reaction. He ignored the insult, but his eyes said he would remember.

After that there was a busy time during which we traded with friendly Indian-beasts Beale had met. Their appearance was less threatening than that of the bold, warlike Comanches. These Zunis were quiet farmers. They gave us much corn for the horses and mules, and our loads became heavier again.

We followed small rivers as often as possible; but even then we got lost at times, although "lost" to an angry Beale and thirsty horses meant nothing to me and my kind. We were equipped to live comfortably almost anywhere. I merely kept my eyes open, always seeking the perfect place, where there would be no sign of *any* kind of men-beasts. When my work on the great road was complete and this place was found—perhaps Beale's

Mojave—I knew my rebellious dreams could be put to rest. I could seize my freedom.

At last we crossed some mysterious, invisible border.

"Hurrah for California!" the soldier-beasts shouted, tossing their caps into the air.

While the caps drifted back down to earth, I glanced around. It looked much as every other piece of desert we'd traversed. I shrugged and waited for the evening's discussion during a comfortable scratching session.

"And this California," I voiced to no one in particular, aiming a hind leg toward a flea on my foreleg. "Is it part of America too?"

"Of course it is, Ali." Seid condescended to answer as he raked his teeth over his withers. "America has many parts and goes on forever. I have heard Beale say so." His neck jerked forward as he paused to preen. "What is more, Beale himself owns vast lands in this California-America. They are north of here—near a place he calls Fort Tejon. We shall all see them, for we will go to Beale's ranch after his labors are finished."

Seid had been almost civil, then spoiled it by adding, "And I shall be in the lead with Beale upon my back!"

"Not for long," Omar muttered as he snapped at flies around his tail.

"You said something, Wrestler?"

Omar growled, flies forgotten. "Of course I said something. Watch your back, Seid, and watch your neck. Pride ill becomes you. One fine day you shall be taken down a notch or two."

Fatinah, who'd been rubbing her flanks on a nearby boulder, shivered, and I walked closer to nudge her cheek and whisper, "Don't worry, Pretty One. It is only foolish talk."

I could make this gesture openly now, for since our Indian adventure, my comrades treated me with greater respect. They almost accepted that Fatinah would be mine when the time was ripe. I was pleased by this acknowledgment but did not take it for granted. Long as this caravan had been, my growth was not yet complete. I must remain wary of the men-beasts, patient with my comrades, and gentle with Fatinah. Above all I must be observant. Our work was almost finished. I must keep a lookout for signs that might lead to my freedom.

Beale called an early halt one afternoon in the foothills of a range of mountains. From his perch atop an ammunition box, he herded the men-beasts together and gave a speech.

"We made it to the finish line. Look back to where we've come from, men. We've done a fine piece of work! After I send my report to Washington City, those congressmen will see that our route is better than the one along the thirty-second parallel to San Diego."

He glanced at my comrades.

"And I think I can truly add that our camels comported themselves better than anyone expected—once we ironed out a few wrinkles in camel husbandry!"

Beale's words were followed by backslapping and roars of laughter.

"Won't regret seein' the tail ends of 'em at last!"

"My nose knows better days is coming!"

I humphed and started to turn around as Beale raised his hand once more.

"End-of-the-road celebration tonight, boys. Break out the last of the whiskey rations. And those fiddles too!"

Nine

In the morning we got a late start. It seems the celebrations did nothing for the heads or stomachs of any of the soldier-beasts. Beale took charge again to split the caravan. He chose Seid and me to go farther west, while he sent Fatinah and the others north to his lands. Although pleased to be so honored, the thought of separation from Fatinah disturbed me. Hi-Jolly, who claimed he was "on the wagon," was fresher than any of the soldiers and did his best to comfort me.

"I will ride upon your back, Ali. Do not worry about your friends. Very soon we will meet again."

Yet it was necessary to catch Fatinah alone before my departure. She looked most fetching in her Comanche trappings. Why was it only in parting that I noticed the gleam in her eye, the silkiness of her nose?

"Be careful, Sweet Cactus Blossom. My thoughts will stay with you until we meet again."

She turned all shyness, averting her eyes from me. "Oh, Ali . . ."

"Take care with the soldiers. And let none of the bulls disturb you with their roughness."

"I think I can look after my virtue, Ali!"

I growled, but at my own ill-chosen words, not at Fatinah. "It is not jealousy, Fatinah, only—"

"Hee-ah!"

Thwack.

"Move out, Ali. Beale's waitin' on you!"

I snapped at the soldier-beast who slapped my flank, but he laughed and jumped away.

"And don't you be spittin' any of that green stuff at me neither, Ali. Not so near the end. Billy Luttig knows your ways after all this time, he does!"

I cast a longing look at Fatinah, but she was already moving north, her nose rope connected to Omar in front, her tail tied to the rope of another wrestler behind. I sighed, lowered myself for Hi-Jolly, and headed up the nearest slope.

We reached the top of a mountain ridge and gazed down. There was something else beyond—a great wave of blueness that stretched from where the land stopped to the horizon. Was it possible that at last we had come to the end of this America?

From his vantage point on my back, Hi-Jolly studied the blueness. "There lies the Pacific Ocean, Ali. They say it rolls clear across to the East. Thank Allah I shall never have to ride upon its waves!" He patted my neck. "It is time I settled down, Ali. Perhaps in this California I will find a wife. A man needs a family, Ali. Henceforth I will shun the cantinas, as Allah would wish. I will save my money and find a worthy woman—"

"Hi-Jolly!"

"Yes, Beale-Sir?"

"Save your breath for the ride down. You've been with camels too long. You act as if they could understand you!"

"Of course they can, Beale-Sir."

Beale laughed. "And keep out of the cantinas down there."

"Yes sir, Beale-Sir. I become a new man in this California." Hi-Jolly brightened.

"Maybe I even find some of the gold that is said to be lying about. . . . Maybe you would share with me some of your great knowledge on the subject?"

Beale snorted and pulled at Seid's rope. "There's no gold lying about. That was mined out almost eight years ago. And besides, the gold was found far north of here—north of Fort Tejon, in the Sierras. I took the first samples back to Washington City myself. It was probably a mistake."

"Why was that, Beale-Sir?"

"Never mind."

We descended the mountain.

Some days later we climbed another piece of those same mountains and came to Fort Tejon, set high in the hills. It was a new army encampment, mostly rows of tents in an open field. Beyond, a small distance away, my comrades waited at Beale's ranch.

I could not tell how much of this land was Beale's, but Seid claimed it went farther than the eye could see in all directions. If that was so, Beale must have been as rich as a pasha. The grazing was good for the fat cattle we saw, and Beale had many servants who ran from every direction at his coming. Why then did he need to be wandering on caravan and pushing rocks around for roads? Men-beasts were a great mystery at times.

As for my own return, Fatinah greeted me cordially, like a brother. *Humph.* It was not the response I expected. And Omar— he kept too close to her for my liking. Alas, there was nothing to be done for the moment.

Hi-Jolly curried me and set me free. I looked forward to resting from the long caravan, to a time of peace when I could appraise what had been accomplished and consider what the future might bring. I hadn't yet found my freedom place, but for now it was enough to have my friends nearby. Enough to have Fatinah close.

Gold! . . . Bright gold! . . . Yellow gold! . . . Gold!

As Beale's ranch prepared for the festival the Infidels called Christmas, we camels were led north, then eastward across a great valley and into another range of mountains. Nearing the white-tipped peaks, Hi-Jolly danced on my back with excitement.

"At last, Ali! The Sierras! The soldiers thought me mad when I volunteered to go alone with you to winter forage." He chuckled. "The soldiers forgot about the *gold.* Even the great Beale shook his head. But he gave me my wages in advance. Now Omar carries the best prospecting gear to be found in Los Angeles."

I swiveled my neck to inspect Hi-Jolly. Some new sickness was surely overtaking

147

him. His eyes had the brightness of fever in them and a look of desire I'd seen only in camels during the mating season. Our cameleer threw back his head and repeated the melody he'd been practicing. His song was wild and undulated like half-forgotten mirages of the East.

Gold! . . . Bright gold! . . . Yellow gold! . . . Gold! I will find you soon, my heart's desire!

Hi-Jolly's incessant chant was hypnotic. Soon our caravan swayed to it. The rhythm even overtook me as we continued into the mountains.

We soon discovered something more interesting than gold. It arrived the first night of our stay in the Sierras. Hi-Jolly had barely completed a small hovel to protect himself during his herding duties when it began to appear from the sky. It was whiter than sand, and it did not sting when it landed on one's eyelashes.

We'd just settled in a ring for the night, not far from Hi-Jolly's small fire, when the substance landed with a small tingle upon my nose. I stuck out my tongue for a taste, but it was gone. Other pieces dropped on my tongue. They were cold and wet, but not unpleasant.

Presently there was whiteness everywhere. I rose to better experience it, then gazed toward Hi-Jolly's hut. He was huddled over his fire, trying to protect the flames.

"Umph?" I grunted in puzzlement.

Hi-Jolly shrugged. "It is not fair, Ali! Beale warned me of this snow, but Allah knows I was unready for it. What will happen if it covers everything? How am I to keep warm?" He rubbed his hands. "I have no thick coat like you! And if the river freezes, it will cover my gold!"

149

Now he was wringing his hands and wailing in earnest. "My gold! It will be covered until spring, and *I* stranded here for months with only camels! Has any Believer deserved such a fate?"

Snow. My skin tingled with the knowing. Surely this was one of Allah's wonders. I settled back to observe its coming through the night.

The morning brought extraordinary changes.

We rested in a small valley between larger mountains. A rushing stream ran not far from our feet. Great trees surrounded us on every side. All was covered with *snow.* The sky was light, but no sun shown. It was a strange light. Perhaps from such a sky more of this snow would fall.

I rose, shaking the blanket of snow from my body. Then I lowered my head to taste it again. It was not a difficult stretch, for the snow came almost to my knees. I opened my mouth. Perhaps snow was like the manna that had fallen from the skies in the deserts of my birthplace in ancient times. The manna that had saved the Israelites from a wicked pharaoh. My teeth closed on a huge clump.

"Faah!" I spit out the coldness.

"What is it, Ali?" Fatinah woke to struggle up from the circle. "Does it taste good?"

"Try it yourself."

She did. "Oh. It is the coldest thing I have ever had on my tongue!" Bewilderment crossed her face. "How shall we eat, Ali? *What* shall we eat?"

I kicked at Allah's wonder. His sense of humor knew no bounds. "Beneath. There is yet food beneath. And on the branches above."

It was an odd time of cold that lasted for many days in our small valley. As there was nowhere for us to go, Hi-Jolly allowed us to graze freely, mostly on the bare, still-supple branches of trees. There were other, stranger trees that stayed green, but the taste of their long, thin spines was bitter. Mercifully the rough-edged cones that fell from them were not unpalatable.

As we browsed around Hi-Jolly, he spent his days in the icy waters of the stream: sifting and staring, sifting and staring as he sloshed gravel in the tin pan of his prospecting kit.

I watched Hi-Jolly turn blue with cold at this strange work. Come first light of day he plunged directly into the stream, wasting no time on our grooming.

"It is better thus," he always repeated. "Your coats will thicken and protect you. I wish to Allah I had such a coat." He tightened the winter robes bound at his waist and stamped his feet with their high work boots, splashing me with icy water.

Then, all of a sudden, would come the chant of his gold song again. The hypnotic rhythm always pulled me back to see what he had found. Hi-Jolly's excitement was hard to fathom as he proudly displayed his finds to me: small shiny shards—smaller than a grain of wheat or oat, rarely as large as a kernel of corn.

"Look, Ali. Fatinah. Look! There *is* gold here, no matter what Beale-Sir has said."

He lovingly placed these insignificant objects inside a small, leathern pouch tied to the belt of his robes. His enthusiasm renewed, Hi-Jolly would set about attacking the stream bottom once more.

Humph. I shook my head as I watched. Apparently there was no such thing as *enough* of this yellow gold.

Relations among my fellow camels remained cordial during this interlude.

Ranging freely, we did not need to disturb one another's ruminations. Real trouble began only after the melting of the snow. By this time Hi-Jolly had sifted the entire length of the stream running through our valley. The pouch at his waist did not yet bulge. He led us back to Fort Tejon.

We arrived at the ranch to find Beale gone. Only his servants and a few soldiers from the fort remained. None of these menbeasts knew what I was coming to understand myself. The bulls had Hi-Jolly's "gold" look in their eyes. It was time to choose mates.

Besides Fatinah there were a half-dozen females in our number, all of them now full grown. The bulls fought furiously for the favors of these few, remorselessly bashing each other to prove they were the strongest and therefore the most worthy of attention.

Exiled

I did not choose to join these displays of power—but neither did Seid. His reticence amazed me, since he had long since attained his maturity. Little by little I understood why he held back: Seid felt he had a chance with Fatinah. Yet Fatinah kept herself aloof, as though the situation were beneath her dignity and notice. Both Seid and I must wait for the fullness of time.

Barely had the mating season passed when Beale returned and chose fourteen of us for another caravan. Thinking it might be a second great road he wished to make, I set off with enthusiasm, having long since wearied of our enforced rest.

We traveled toward Los Angeles, then east across the desert. But Beale had brought none of his surveyors along, and our job proved nothing more than bearing burdens where horses and mules could not easily go. Yet something wonderful did come of the trip: Beale took us through that place of which I had been dreaming—the Mojave.

Excitement gripped me. I saw sifting dunes of sand mirroring those of my native land. There were no men-beasts either—not even Indians—aside from those in our caravan. I heard Beale himself say he chose this route only because it was early spring. No human in his right mind would come this way in the heat of summer.

I kept careful track of the conjunction of the stars in the sky above me, knowing that I must find my way back one day. Alas, the passage through this trackless land went too quickly. Soon we broke through to rock and scrub and the Colorado River. There, unexpectedly, Beale ordered our return to California with Hi-Jolly and a few soldiers.

Seid, still Beale's favorite, reported on this surprising turn of events.

"Beale leaves for the same Washington

City where Major-Sir disappeared. I fear I shall not see him again. If only he had taken me with him. He knows I am superior to a horse! Why does he abandon me like this?"

"Afraid you'll have to do some real work again, Seid, like the rest of us?" Omar spit out.

Seid raised his neck with dignity. "I have always carried my fair share when required, Wrestler."

Omar laughed in Seid's face. "You'd rather not have it required. Isn't that it? Beale's made you soft with his pats on your flanks and his compliments—"

Seid lunged for Omar, but I saw it coming and swiftly stepped between them to take the blow. "Have a little patience, Omar. You were once a favorite of your mistress. Surely you mourned her passing?"

His answer was a painful bite to my hindquarters. "Omar mourns no man-beast.

Omar makes his own destiny."

The Pehlevan spun away, while Fatinah approached to lick my wound.

Poor Seid was desolate for the entire return caravan. We told him he should never put his faith in a man-beast, but he was deaf to our advice. We returned to the ranch near Fort Tejon and were set loose in a great field amid Beale's cattle. Then we were forgotten.

Ten

Beale and the army forgot us. Even Hi-Jolly forgot us. But there were still men-beasts at Fort Tejon.

Grazing in a field one day, I observed two servants furtively approaching us around the edge of a hill. They were swarthy and thick. I did not care for the sly look in their eyes—or the ominous sticks and ropes they carried. I bellowed a warning to Fatinah and Seid. Fatinah loped away, but Seid ignored my call, still deep in mourning for his Beale.

Fool! Yet I delayed my own escape in concern for him.

My instincts were correct. The loop of a lasso used for untrained horses twirled through the air to settle around his neck. Seid glanced up and blinked.

"Fight!" I bellowed.

Seid shrugged, too spiritless to care. Another lasso sped my way, but I easily dodged it. As it fell to the ground, I stamped on its loop and grasped the rope between my teeth. With a running leap I tore the entire length from the hands of its owner, flinging it into a nearby thicket of thorn.

"Caramba! This second humpback will not be easy, Manuel. Will not the mines settle for one?"

"More than one is required, Caesar. The silver we're offered is for more."

The ruffians tightened the rope around

Seid's neck and approached him, sticks at the ready. I remained a distance off, teeth bared.

"Fight, Seid! Fight for liberty! These men-beasts mean you harm!"

Seid swung his neck lethargically. "What does it matter? Without Beale one bondage is as good as another."

Doom closed in on my friend as the servants poked him with their sticks.

"Has this one health, Manuel? They must be strong to carry the silver ore. Garcia said the mines kill the pack animals too easily. . . ."

"Garcia may learn for himself after the coins cross our palms. Hurry, Caesar. The camels must be gone before Beale returns. A few runaways can be excused."

At the sound of Beale's name, at the promise of his return, Seid found new life. He jerked his neck and swung at the one called Caesar. I closed in to attack Manuel but was distracted by another sound behind me. Fearing ambush, I spun to find a raven-haired child-beast staring at us, eyes wide. He had appeared from nowhere and now moved forward, limping with the aid of a thick staff.

"Papá! You must not steal Señor Beale's camels!"

"Stop your tongue, Tito. My business is none of yours."

"I will tell this to him, Papá. He has given us a home and a garden for Mamá."

"Silence!" Manuel ceased belaboring Seid with his stick and aimed it instead at the crippled child. Tito dropped his crutch and dodged it as adroitly as I had. With his father distracted and Caesar ropeless, this was the moment to attack.

"Fight!" I roared at Seid. "Fight if you wish to see your Beale again!"

Renewed, Seid took on Caesar—and I

the luckless Papá. It had been too long since I'd had a salty hand in my mouth or a bulbous nose. Legs flailing, neck and teeth thrust forward, pictures from my childhood in the camel market flashed before me. I had been slipping into a lethargy almost as lethal as Seid's.

"Never submit," my mother had said.

I kicked my feet out again, but already it was finished. Manuel and Caesar were hopping away like jackrabbits. Their hair and clothing were askew, and they bore bloodied testimony to our prowess. I grinned at Seid, and he laughed back.

"Beale will never return to find me gone, Ali. I will fight for him!"

"It's time, Seid. You have slumbered too long."

I glanced at the child-beast. He stood unafraid, seriously considering what had just taken place.

"*Bueno.* Papá will be angry, but he has been saved from losing another job. I must tell Mamá." Reaching painfully for his fallen crutch, Tito began his struggle back to the ranch house. Then he stopped to crook his neck back at us.

"How wonderful you are!"

Now on guard, the strongest among us took turns watching over our herd. Seid grasped command of this duty. I allowed him to, for it returned the self-esteem lost with Beale's departure. His renewed cockiness offended no one but Omar, who spit bitter bile each time he saw Seid perched in dominance on a rise above us.

"Silver mines" entered our conversation. It became a term equated with disaster. Had not mines existed even in the time of the Ancients? Had not both slave-beasts and camels disappeared into them forever?

Exiled

Tito's papá did not return. Tito did. We welcomed the child-beast as a defender of our kind. Fatinah trotted to him and nuzzled him as if he were a firstborn runt, needful of much extra care. Soon she even had me fussing over the urchin. We lowered our legs willingly to young Tito, carrying him freely across Beale's lands, where his own legs were too painful to take him.

The child-beast brought rewards, too, since Tito spoke to us as openly as Hi-Jolly. He carried gossip from the ranch house— and sometimes a rare sweet root from the kitchen where his mother labored. This root he halved with great solemnity and ritual before sharing it with Fatinah and myself.

Thus the seasons passed once, and once again. The females gave birth to young ones—all but Fatinah. She gazed upon these little ones with longing and often took part in their care and training, just as she looked

after Tito. The little ones gave her the hon-
orific of "aunt." But it was not the same as
"mother." Fatinah knew this. Very soon she
must choose among the three of us who vied
for her attentions.

Yes, it was still three. Though Omar had
won another female, he felt that a Pehlevan
of his stature required more than one wife.
Only a harem would do for Omar.

All these many seasons I had enjoyed the
lands of Beale around Fort Tejon. They were
pleasant enough lands. They grew hot and
dry in summer, and in winter the occasional
snows were bracing. But here it was too easy
to allow time to drift into nothingness. It was
too easy to forget my dreams of total freedom. I longed for a land made for a camel: a
land of thistle and scrub and sand dunes
across which I could gallop. A land that held
a certain mystery—if not the mystery of the

Ancients, at least that of a vast void that only Allah could create for the sheer pleasure and amusement of creating it. I hoped the Mojave would be such a place.

It could be mine, now, too. I knew the stars to follow, checking them as I did each night. Yet I held back. What I waited for, hoped for, was Fatinah. But I dared not voice the need even to myself.

The Infidels had given Hi-Jolly his own freedom, but he was equally unsure of what to do with it. Maybe he missed his homeland, too, for that second winter he sought me out. I watched him come across the open field, his feet crunching on the lightly frosted grass. If it was not for my sense of smell, I would not have recognized him. His robes were gone. He looked even smaller, and perhaps a little sad, in Infidel working clothes. He had no need to chase me. When he called my name, I waited.

"Ali." His black curls, flecked now with white, rubbed against my neck. "Ali. What is to become of us? More than ever we are strangers in a strange land." He patted my nose and showed the tip of a root vegetable he'd hidden behind his back. I snatched it.

"I married, Ali. I have become a family man. I even have a small daughter, and another child is on the way. Yet this woman, my wife—by Allah, she is a hard one! Always it is work, work! 'There is no time for the cantinas, Hi-Jolly,' she says. 'There is no time for dreams of gold! Go back to the army,' she tells me. 'Stop talking of your stupid camels and make some money from them. If they are so wonderful, why can't they make some money for us?'"

The sweet root was gone, but he still clung to me. I sniffed his garments for more.

"I swear by Allah, Ali. I swear if it were not for that sea voyage, I would return to

Egypt." He stroked my back. "No. It's not to be. So. I make another plan. Perhaps this one will work."

"Umph?"

Hi-Jolly explained.

"I have sent letters to Washington City, to Beale-Sir. I have asked him to allow me to carry the mails over the mountains, using some of you. Messages between Los Angeles and the forts. Maybe something will come of it. I wait."

Then he was gone, and mating season arrived.

It was a cold day. The skies were gray. Rains would be coming.

It began innocently enough.

Fatinah rose from her place of sleep near Seid, Omar, and me. She bid us all a gracious good morning as she strolled off to graze. Omar swung his head and followed her with

169

his eyes, inadvertently bumping Seid.

"Clumsy Wrestler!" muttered Seid. "So much wasted training. So little grace."

"You've had superior training with Beale, I assume?" snarled Omar.

"Beale is a gentleman. He knows how to pick the finest mounts!" Seid shot back.

"And knows how to desert them, too, these many moons."

"Beale has not deserted me! He shall return! With harness of silver! He promised me!"

Seid should have stopped there, but he never did know when to stop.

"Then I shall have Beale and Fatinah too! We will look well together, Fatinah and I. She in her beads, I in my silver."

"You live in dreams," growled Omar. "Fatinah will choose only the mightiest for her children. *I* am the mightiest."

"It is true you are large, but in your

hindquarters, not your head, from which the thinking comes! Be satisfied with the wife you already have."

They were on their feet now, moving away from the rest of us as they jostled each other. Then, before my very eyes, their jostlings and snide remarks sparked into something more intense, more vicious.

I searched quickly for Fatinah, to see if I could protect her from the inevitable. This time she did not avert her gaze from where she stood. This time she stared with fascination.

I strode to her. "Fatinah. Please. Let me escort you away from this."

"No, Ali. I must stay."

It was true then. Finally she was ready for a mate.

Seid and Omar paced around each other in circles that became smaller and smaller, all the while violently flicking their tails and roaring out challenges. These challenges vibrated through the hills, returning in echoes. The sky grew darker still.

Seid made the first lunge with his neck. Omar deftly sidestepped him, then shot out with his own neck, delivering a solid blow. Seid ignored this blow that would have stopped a smaller bull. He thrust again, mouth open wide, and managed a vicious bite to Omar's rear flanks. Omar spun, raised his front legs, and kicked out wildly. Seid's body accepted this punishment, too, and he swung yet again with his neck. Omar blocked with his own neck, receiving some of the powerful jolt. They both stepped back to regroup.

Next to me, Fatinah was shaking. "I know this must happen, Ali. But it is hard. Very hard. Especially when my heart lies elsewhere."

I caught her eyes. Truth lay within them. She wanted *me*!

Enough waiting. With a soaring heart, I sped toward the two bulls. But there was no chance to enter the battle. No chance for intervention. None. They were locked together. The rutting ritual had become mortal combat.

Necks and legs were intertwined. Teeth grasped anything that could be bitten. Breath came in gasps as they heaved against each other. Suddenly Omar pulled free. With one mighty lunge of his neck, he disabled Seid, following the move with a mightier kick. Seid fell and lay sprawled on his side.

He looked up, panting. "Perhaps your training was of some use, Wrestler."

"*Who* is victor?" snarled Omar.

"*You* are, Omar."

"Yes. *Now and forever.*"

I halted on the edge of the battleground,

waiting for Omar to back off now that he had won. Seid could console himself with dreams of his Beale. I would confront Omar. But Omar did not back off. His eyes were red with hatred, his mouth flecked with foam. He lifted one forefoot over Seid's head.

"*No,* Omar!"

My protest was too late. Omar's foot smashed into Seid's skull, crushing it.

Seid twitched, then was still.

A keening wail rose from the throats of Fatinah and the other females. My heart plunged through four stomachs. My friend was gone. My moment had come. I stepped forward.

"Murderer!"

Omar's head rose from his kill. His eyes were still clouded with fury. "Dare you say that again, Ali?"

"*Murderer!* You are not worthy of Fatinah!"

Exiled

I parried his neck thrust, then hove into battle with all my being.

Forward, back. Do not think of the rain now falling.

Forward, back, forward, **strike.**

Do not think of the thunder in the heavens.

Kick.

Thrust.

Think of Fatinah. Think of Seid, so ignominiously defeated.

Lunge.

Bite.

Do not think of the ache within. The pain and sorrow. Thrust yet again.

Strike.

Strike with the fury of righteousness.

Strike. *With the heat of revenge.*

Strike. *For the mate ordained to me. . . .*

The enemy is down.

Think of Seid. Think of Fatinah.

My foot raised in anger must be lowered.

I lower it, but not upon Omar's head.

Walk away, into the rain. Walk past the body of Seid, my passionate, foolish orphan friend. Walk off into the hills.

No.

Race.

Race the winds of the storm. Race the bolts of lightning, the booms of thunder. . . . Yet there is a sound behind me, not of the storm.

Stop?

For a moment only. Turn. See Fatinah, following. Following more freely and with more will than ever before.

"Fatinah."

Her nose touches mine. Her tongue cleanses my bloodied face.

"Ali. At last it is time for us."

Eleven

It was almost like the old road-building days carrying sacks of mail for Hi-Jolly. How good to put my strength to use on caravan. All was good—except Seid was not with us. Not even his bones. A curious end, indeed, for a camel.

Shortly after Seid's murder, soldiers carrying shovels arrived from the fort. We followed them to the field where Seid was buried and watched them sling earth from his mound.

"Ain't that Beale sumpin' else though?"

the first one said. "Spendin' all this time and money on a camel? Imagine wantin' his bones sent to that there Smithsonian Museum in Washington City!"

"Easy to be sumpin' else, Riley, when you ain't doing the digging. My, but this critter's gonna smell ripe!"

"Wisht Beale woulda thought of this afore the burying, George."

"He was off in Washington. You know that. They sent him a telegram. *Jehosephat.* Can you imagine. A telegram clear across three thousand miles for a *camel*?"

They dug deeper. Was it proper and correct to disturb a burial place? I thought of what had happened to those who knowingly desecrated the tombs of the Ancients in my homeland. Such violators were cursed—in life and in the afterlife. I backed off.

Then the stench came.

The soldier-beasts tied handkerchiefs

across their noses and continued. I crept up again—

"*Scat!* We oughta just start with a live one, George, like this'n. Be a sight easier to strip down."

George eyed me. I bared my teeth.

"No, Riley, give Beale what he wants. They'll have a fine old time rebuildin' the brute though."

Riley pulled up his nose rag and spat. "Won't be the same creature atall without the smell."

They roared at their humor. Rebuilt? Seid? How could something whose spirit had gone be rebuilt, I wondered? Was this another joke of Allah's?

There was much time to consider these new mysteries of life and death as I steadily traversed mountain trails. The leather satchels of mail on my back did not burden me.

What *did* was Fatinah's absence. Without her I had no one with whom to share my thoughts. Her time was nearly ripe for the birth of our firstborn.

Not even Omar was along. Since his abominable deed, he'd been separated from the rest of us and shunned by all—especially Hi-Jolly, whose reaction to the news of Seid's violent end had been explosive.

"Sell him to the silver mines! Omar's punishment should be long and hard!"

"Humph!" I spat vehement agreement. But no one came from the silver mines. Omar grazed in splendid isolation while we remaining bulls continued to work.

Our current mail caravan made me nervous. The stopover in Los Angeles seemed interminable. Finally we were homeward bound again, up the parched hills toward Tejon, and Fatinah. Would the young one already have arrived? Half of me wished it so, that the waiting would be over. The other half wished to be present at the moment of birth to give Fatinah the support she deserved.

During these days just before father-hood, I thought long and hard about my own father. Why hadn't he been present on my arrival into the world? Although my mother never discredited him, at times she had seemed wistful. Perhaps my father's need for total freedom had been greater than his need for his family.

It could never be so with me. Had I not had many opportunities to free myself on these trips? Hi-Jolly was very trusting of me and allowed me advantages not given the others. Yet great as was my desire to be free, greater still was the knowledge that this freedom would be nothing without those I loved. Fatinah. The little one still

181

unborn. When the time was ripe, we would find freedom together.

The last few miles into Beale's valley were endless—and still there was more delay for me to bear while the mail was delivered at the fort. Anxious to be on my way, I pawed the earth and snorted instead of resting with the others. The only diversion from my frustration was the army camp itself.

It had grown different since my first arrival long moons past. Wooden barracks stood where tents had once covered the hillside. Yet it seemed as if the very same soldiers lounged around the well, pumping water and splashing one another in the heat. Curious how most men-beasts were indistinguishable from one another. . . .

Under a spindly, lone tree, I watched as they received their letters. I knew this ritual well. At the sound of a horn, soldier-beasts dropped everything and stood at attention.

Those who received the flimsy envelopes showed hope and excitement on their faces. Those who did not turned sullen, using their crude soldier language and kicking things. Some would even kick us, the camels who were merely the messengers. Did they believe violence would bring them a letter on our next trip? I would rather eat such a letter than be its bearer to inconsiderate beasts. Alas, I never could learn to decipher the bird scratchings on these papers.

Long after the mail call, Hi-Jolly rested by the well, pumping water over his head every few minutes. My frustrations grew. Leaving the shade of the tree, I headed for the cameleer and grumbled at him. No response. Taking matters into my own teeth, I bent my head to grasp at his sleeve. He swatted me.

"By Allah, you hound me like a demon, Ali. Cannot you let a man rest for a moment?"

"Umph!"

I mouthed his entire arm and dragged him up. The soldier-beasts were watching; some laughing, some astounded.

"That there camel has got hisself some-place he'd rather be, Hi-Jol!"

"Bet he's got a girlfriend back at Beale's!"

Hi-Jolly shook himself free of my grasp and slapped his head. "Where is my thinking? Of course! He has himself a wife, and she is due to give birth."

"Aw, come on. Ain't no camel smart enough to know that."

"*Ali* is smart enough." The cameleer turned to me. "Please forgive me, my friend Ali. We will leave immediately."

We did.

We arrived at Beale's ranch just before sunset. Tito was waiting for a ride, but for once I ignored him. Hi-Jolly loosed me, and I set off in search of Fatinah.

Exiled

She was standing by a distant fence away from the others. She had grown larger than I had ever seen her. My thoughts settled into one single sigh of relief. *I am in time.*

"Fatinah." I touched her nose, ran my neck along her swollen side.

"Was your caravan hard, Ali?"

"Only in worry for you."

She nodded. "I waited. I told the young one he must wait too."

"He?"

"I am sure. He is most impatient. My stomachs are sore with his kicking, his desire to be free."

"Tell him he may come now. His father is here."

As the moon rose, two small forelegs appeared in the birth opening, with a head between them. Fatinah gave a great shudder, and the rest of the body followed. Soon a small, furry bundle lay heaving on the grass—humming with pleasure to be in the world at last!

Fatinah was exhausted but also elated. She nosed the bundle, prompting it to its feet. There it stood, wobbling, before it let out a piercing baby cry.

"May I?" I wanted very much to inspect this new being I had helped to create.

Fatinah smiled. "Quickly. Come and meet your son. He is very hungry and will not put up with a curious father for long."

"*A son?* Truly?" I stepped over and smelled the little one. He was warm and soft. I let out a vast roar of wonder and delight. My son screamed.

"Ali! How could you frighten Seid so?" She pushed me away, then nudged the baby toward her milk.

"*Seid?*"

"Do you not approve? I thought long

about the proper name. It seemed right. This Seid will not be an orphan."

"Yes." I turned the name over in my mind. "Yes. It is good."

I backed away, then sank onto the grass to thank Allah and to watch over my family. It had been a long day, but a good one.

"Father!"

Insistent nudgings roused me from my sleep.

"Father!"

The nudgings turned into playful leaps onto my back and much snapping of young jaws.

"What is it, Seid? The sun is not yet up, and I am weary from my work!"

"But it was your last caravan, Father. You told me so. Hi-Jolly, he told me so, too, when he came to say good-bye. You promised there would be time to play when your work was finished."

"When the sun is up, Seid."

"The sky grows red, Father. Don't waste the day in sleep!"

Groaning, I rose. This fathering business had more to it than met the eye. Young Seid, but a few moons old, had energy in excess of what I could ever remember possessing.

"Today we run, Father. You promised. Today you teach me to gallop. I will be a great racer like my grandfather."

"Yes, but not too far. You'll get hungry."

Seid jiggled impatiently as he glanced at his mother, still sleeping. "Mother will follow us. Mother always knows when I'm hungry."

So I ran with my son, remembering my own milk days. I was sad that he could not be taught the mysteries of the Ancients the way I had been. Neither would he see

188

minarets and pyramids piercing the sky. But
I could tell him of such things. And were
there not other mysteries to be learned in
this land of America? *Indians,* and *snow* and
prickly pears. There were compensations.

Young Seid's milk days flew by. One morning Fatinah was still kissing and tonguing
and nursing him, and it seemed only the
next when it was time for him to taste his
first solid food. Not the little nibbles he'd
playfully taken of the cattle grass but real
camel food. Fatinah was anxious.

"It is so soon, Ali."

"Nonsense, Fatinah. You have nurtured
him nearly twelve moons. My own mother
went dry in my tenth moon."

She bit her lip. "But will he like the food
here? There is not much thorn, or even
mesquite. And——"

"Stop worrying, Fatinah. I went

exploring yesterday. I discovered a small prickly pear hidden away that no one else has found. We will take him there this morning."

"Ali, how perfect!" Then she began fussing again. "But will such a delicacy spoil him for the thorn when we do find it?"

"He is a camel, Fatinah. And our son." I smiled proudly. "Young Seid will know what he likes."

He did. I watched him edge up to the prickly pear I'd chosen. He gazed at it for a long moment, then moved nearer and sniffed it. His nose wrinkled.

"It doesn't smell like Mother's milk, Father."

Fatinah smiled on one side of me but said nothing.

"It is not your mother's milk, son, but you cannot drink that forever. There are other sweetnesses in life." I gave him a little nudge. "Go ahead. Try it."

Obediently Seid opened his small jaw, took a little leap forward, and nipped at the cactus. Tentatively, very tentatively, his teeth closed down, and he began to chew. He raised the long lashes on his eyelids and gave me a startled look. Then he jumped back for another nip, this time larger. In short order the prickly pear was gone.

I glanced at Fatinah. "You see?"

Poor Fatinah was bereft. She'd lost her baby.

"Never mind," I whispered in her ear. "A daughter would be nice too."

Already Seid was running circles around both of us. "That was great, Father! Now I'd like to taste some thorn. Surely you can find me some thorn?"

Matters were not so calm in the world of the men-beasts. After the army ended Hi-Jolly's mail caravan, someone came officially to choose a few of us to work in the silver mines of Nevada. Tito limped out to warn us.

"Ali! Fatinah! Take your baby and flee! The owner of the silver mine himself approaches!" I bent so Tito could climb on my back and bellowed a warning to the others. My family ran to the top of a hill and looked down. A great, shaggy man-beast soon appeared on horseback, followed by half a score of Beale's retainers. I swiveled my neck to give Tito a questioning look.

"Alas, Señor Beale has written we must allow this thing. I know not why. It is his work, not that of my papá."

I grunted as I watched. The owner of the mine seemed more knowledgeable about our kind than Manuel and Caesar had been. Also more organized. Omar—free among us once more as the memories of men-beasts weakened—tried to take on

Seid's role as protector. Alas, our memories of Seid remained strong. The herd was split between hatred of Omar and fear of the silver mine. Six camels were captured, two of them wrestlers. It was a sorry sight to see them being led off. I bawled out a farewell.

"What's happening, Father? Why do those men-beasts take away my uncles? And if it's to a bad place, shouldn't Omar be included?"

"Yes, Omar should be included!" I spat. Fatinah gave me a nudge, and I tried to control my anger. "It is the way of the world, son." I sighed. How better to explain? "We have been sheltered too long. Our instincts have become dulled." I bit savagely at a nearby bush, while Tito tried to give me a comforting pat.

"Be calm, friend Ali." Tito's words were soft. "They only needed six. I heard them say as much. You and your family are safe."

Safe! If six could be taken so easily, others would disappear too. What was happening with Beale in Washington City that he
would allow this atrocity? Why were we not
being worked usefully for his benefit? Or
that of the army, which had uprooted us to
begin with? At least the making of roads, the
carrying of mail for Hi-Jolly, had been honorable labor.

Humph.

Soon after, several others of my kind
were taken to Los Angeles, never to return.
But the rest of the herd remained with
Beale's placid cattle—dumb animals who
cared nothing for either the worlds of men-
beasts or camels, who cared only for the
green grass that fattened them for slaughter.
The questions in my mind grew.

Seeking answers, I began to frequent the
ranch buildings to learn bits of information
Tito may have missed. Although my feelings

for the men-beasts were ambiguous, their doings still fascinated me. Also the ranch cook often left amusing morsels to cool on the porch. In such a way had I discovered a thing called *apple pie*. Even the thought of that sweetness was enough to send my senses reeling—and to make me forget the broom wielded by Tito's own mamá when she discovered me licking the last juices from her empty pie tin!

Thinking I might find another of these pies for Fatinah and young Seid, I strolled often toward the kitchen, nonchalantly, as if I were the landowner, not Beale. This was how I learned of the event called *The Civil War*.

It was the day when Beale finally returned from the East, speaking of a new sultan named Lincoln and of his own new position as something called *Surveyor General of California*. Beale was excited as he dismounted in front of his staff and quickly

195

gave them the news of the country.

"Yes, we are at war. Yes, Texas has gone with the South. Will there be trouble here? Not at Rancho El Tejon, never fear. But on the coast, perhaps. If the South can spare ships to round the Cape and attack our coastline."

By this time I was walking forward boldly, and Beale stopped short to recognize me. "Ali, is it? You're still here then? But not for long, my friend. I've orders to sell you off. Neither the North nor the South knows what to do with camels in time of war. A pity. I've heard your comrades in Arabia make wonderful cavalry mounts."

Then he turned away, dismissing me, and marched into his house.

I took the news directly back to Fatinah.

"There is unrest among the men-beasts," I began. "There may be fighting."

"Fighting?" Her glance swung instantly

to Seid, who was cheerfully cropping grass like one of the cattle.

"There is more." I told her all I knew. Finally she looked up at me.

"The fighting is bad. But the selling might be worse, I think. You yourself were separated from your mother at a camel market."

"Yes." I nodded gravely. The memory would always be branded within me.

"Perhaps it is time to search for that freedom you've been speaking of for so long, Ali."

"But we've been happy here . . ."

"True." Her eyes took in the hilly fields. "Yes, we have. Yet sometimes even my feet long for the feel of sand beneath them."

The feel of sand beneath my feet. Fatinah's words made the feeling sweep over me again—that old longing, stronger than ever. Not so much for the sand itself as for what came with it: no control, unfettered by the burdens of men-beasts. I grunted. "It may be hard, Fatinah."

"I am strong, and Seid is quite old enough to travel."

"It is so." I made a decision. "There is no more honorable work waiting for us here. We must blaze our own trails."

"Tonight?"

I considered. "No. At the new moon. The stars will be brighter to guide us. And the darkness will better disguise us."

Freedom

*Enter ye here
in Peace and Security.*

XV, 46
QUR'AN

Twelve

The new moon appeared at last, and none
too soon. The owner of a circus had arrived on
Beale's land that very afternoon. He spent
some hours poking at us with a whip the size of
which I hadn't seen since my days with
Abdullah. I did not like the way this rough
man-beast looked at Fatinah and my son.
Neither did Tito, who balanced nervously
against a fence post of the corral into which
we'd been herded.

"What'd you think, Beale? This pair . . ."
The circus man flicked his whip toward

Fatinah and Seid. "They'd look handsome in a parade, eh? Babies always go over big with the crowds. And I could charge a pretty penny for rides. Maybe even paint up the youngster to work with my clowns."

"What about the father?" Beale pointed me out, though I was hovering near enough to my family for any fool to make the connection.

"Forget him. Two's enough. He'd only be another mouth to feed."

"I must warn you, Miller. Ali is quite attached to his family—"

"Humbug! What do camels know of family? Let's talk price, Beale." He dragged Beale off toward the ranch house.

Beale paused to give orders to a servant. "Keep the camels in the corral for the night. Miller may want a third after all, and it will save the trouble of rounding them up."

I groaned with dismay. I'd waited too long. Seeking a way to escape, I inspected the posts of the corral. They were high and would not be as easy to breach as that of the Indian-beasts so long ago. Distressed, I swung wildly around—and saw Tito beckoning to me. Going to him, I lowered my neck and mouth to his outstretched arms and accepted his caress.

"Never will I let that Miller take away Fatinah and your son!" he whispered in my ear. "Sooner I would free all of you—" He stopped. "But then I would lose all my good friends—especially you, Ali."

Tito sighed deeply, and I whuffled in sympathy. This child-beast was not like the others. He understood. As well as Hi-Jolly. Was this how my kind had been subjugated in the beginning? By men-beasts who had kindness within them? Yet he would still prefer my subjugation to attain his own needs.

Tito's next words proved me wrong.

"It will hurt, Ali. Very much will it hurt.

But for you I will do it. Tonight, very late, I will creep from my bed and open the gate. Have your family ready. I cannot wait long or my father may find me . . . and beat me."

I nuzzled the young one's face. If he could live on thorns it might be a temptation to carry him with us. What a pity he could not. The Mojave would not be kind to a child-beast like him. I wickered as I watched him stumble away with his stick.

"What is happening, Ali?"

I turned to my mate. "Tito will help us tonight, Fatinah. Else all is lost. We must prepare."

I nudged Fatinah and young Seid past the other camels to a water trough and ordered them to drink their fill.

"But I'm not thirsty, Father," complained my son. "It's only two days since I drank—"

"Drink! We go into the desert where water will not come to us as easily as here. And I am not yet sure of the plants we'll find on our way, how much moisture they might contain."

Young Seid did my bidding while I studied Fatinah. "Earlier today, before the Miller-beast's coming, did you lick at the salt block as I directed?"

"Of course, Ali."

Satisfied, I lowered my own head to the trough. In a matter of moments I had emptied it. Shaking the last few drops of water from my mouth, I inspected my family. They were sleek and healthy, their humps full and firm. Pray Allah they would remain so. I looked up at the sky, which had darkened into night.

"Soon, with Tito's help, we will go. Silently. As silently as from the Comanche camp."

"Oh! Will we see wild Indians on our adventure, Father? I'd love a headdress like Mother's!"

I gave my son a stern look. "Pray daily to

Allah that we meet no such Indian-beasts. They would make short work of an untried yearling like you."

"But, Father—"

"Enough! We will leave over the hills to the north, then circle slowly around the edges of Beale's lands till we have reached the east. Thus we shall continue till the Mojave meets us."

"How long will it take, Father, to find this Mojave and the freedom you're always talking about?"

"Hush now. No need for the others to know. But to answer you fairly, son, it will take as long as safety requires."

The darkness was half gone when I caught the shadow of Tito shuffling his way past the ranch buildings to the corral. I twitched my ears and humphed softly to myself. Would the other camels notice his coming? No. They were sleeping peacefully in their ring, knowing

Miller had little interest in any of them.

I watched the urchin-beast more seriously now, almost holding my breath. His progress was so slow. So painful. I could see the concentration on his thin, dark face as he attempted his job with speed and silence.

I nudged Fatinah and young Seid toward the corral gate.

"Why is he taking so long, Father?"

I cuffed Seid with my head. "Be patient and never speak ill of this child-beast!" I hissed. "Tonight he becomes our savior."

Finally Tito was at the gate, loosening the latch. It creaked open slowly, excruciatingly. It seemed the sky itself shrieked with the sound. Yet no one else heard.

Tito leaned hard on his stick. There were beads of sweat on his brow. "Come, Ali. Come, Fatinah. You must go. I will pray to the Virgin for you."

I licked his face, removing the salty sweat.

It was the sweetest I ever tasted of man-beast. Then we were out of the corral, my family and I. *Free.*

We slipped away, walking steadily over the hills of Beale's lands. A single, meandering fence marked its borders. I split this fence with one blow of my neck, so Fatinah could step gracefully over its shards. Young Seid, however, turned up his nose at such an easy escape. He leaped over an unbroken section, then challenged me with a grin. What could I do? I backed up a few paces and followed his example.

My son laughed aloud. "So. You aren't as old as the Ancients you're always telling me about, Father. Yet."

I gave him a clip on his rear flank. His impertinence grew daily. It wasn't a hard blow, though, and my son and I both hid our smiles. So we continued through the night, reveling in our liberty, using small jokes to make us forget the sadness on Tito's face.

As dawn approached, I turned east. We were still in the soft, bald hills of the range that Beale's servants called the Tehachapi. After clearing them, it would be another week's journey before we reached the center of the Mojave and our new home. But for now my family needed to rest.

I selected a place of harbor carefully—a tiny hummock between two hills. It had several large boulders and a few struggling trees behind which we could hide. Fatinah and young Seid fell into an immediate slumber. My intentions were to keep watch over them, yet my head drooped. . . .

"Father!"

I awoke with a start. The sun was high and bright in the sky. "What is it, Seid?"

"Sound, Father. Horses."

I nodded. "Good job, son," I murmured.

"Be still."

The wait was not long. Soon horses came at a trot over the crest of a nearby hill. I could see their riders: Beale, and that circus-beast, and a few of Beale's retainers. They slowed to a stop, their eyes following the ground, their voices floating over the distance to us.

"No more trace of them varmints, Mr. Beale, sir. The last spoor was over a mile back."

"Where in blazes have they gotten to?" growled the circus-beast. "I want my camels, Beale. I paid you hard cash for them last night!"

"You paid the U.S. government, Miller." Beale's voice was a slow drawl. "And not nearly so much as they're worth."

"Nevertheless, I want them! I've planned my next season's show around them! How in the devil's name did they jump that corral anyway?"

I wish I could have seen Beale's face.

Exiled

Surely it had that familiar, slightly amused look on it. His answer proved me right.

"You'll just have to return and select some of the others, Miller. Ali has had the run of my spread for several years. He never chose to leave before. Perhaps he didn't wish to lose his family to you. Maybe he just didn't care for the set of your trousers. Who knows? But I wouldn't put either past him!"

"You dare to credit a mere animal with such intelligence?"

"It has crossed my mind on occasion, Miller. And if you're seriously contemplating living with any of my other camels, it wouldn't hurt to take more trouble to understand them."

"Nonsense! Tripe!" Miller spat. But he pivoted his horse around. "Let them go. I've wasted enough time on this wild camel chase."

Slowly the horses retreated west, back across the mountains. I turned to see Fatinah watching with our son.

"Beale had possibilities." I smiled. "A pity for him that he didn't study us further. Had he chosen Omar as a mount rather than his horse, we would have been discovered at once."

"Omar would have exposed us?"

"Without question. His nose would have found us, and his black heart would have betrayed us."

"Allah is still watching over us, Ali."

"Yes, Fatinah. He is."

The hills were becoming harder and steeper. I judged it necessary to give young Seid the training that Beale's lands had never required.

"On this next slope, son, do as I do. Going up a steep incline, it's always knees down, push with your hind legs."

Seid folded his gangly front legs beneath him and scrabbled ineffectively with his rear ones. *"Umph.* Like this, Father?"

I hid a smile. "The body is willing but the execution is somewhat deficient. Watch me again."

Slowly we worked our way to the top of the pass. Seid looked down the far side. "If I lower my knees here, Father, I shall certainly slide on my nose to the bottom!"

Fatinah giggled. "Your sense of smell would be blunted for days. Watch your father."

"Going down, keep your forelegs high, as in walking, but lower your rear legs. It breaks the descent."

Seid tried. I couldn't say that his nose would remain bruiseless, but he was learning fast. At the bottom we paused to browse among a few scattered bushes before continuing on our way. By the middle of the night we were another ten or twelve man-beast miles from Beale's lands. I called a halt. Starting on the morrow, we could travel at an easier pace during the light.

Our exodus continued, leading us each day farther out of the mountains, easing us into the dry, barren lands of the high desert.

I knew we were safe when we stumbled upon the first salt pan. In the heat of the afternoon's sun, it shimmered like a mirage in the deserts of my own country. My mother had spoken of mirages, and my old friend Seid, too, from his true caravan days. I thought of his words now. "From a distance it looks like a great expanse of water, Ali. But your nose will tell you it is not so. The real desert has many tricks such as this to play. Only the men-beasts fall for them."

We walked closer and tasted the salt. It was pure. Fatinah smiled at me. "How useful, Ali. Whenever we have a longing for salt, we can return."

"True." I glanced up at the relentlessly burning sun. "And no man-beast will disturb us. The great heat of these days—and the coldness of the nights—is not congenial to them."

Young Seid was not equally impressed. "Is this all there is, Father? Surely there's more. Where are the sand dunes you promised me?"

"Have a little patience, for Allah's sake. Look around you. All that you see, all that is beyond what you can see, is ours. Ours to criss-cross with roads as in the deserts of the East." My eyes closed with the beauty of the dream. Roads that would become honorable and ancient in their time—to be sung about and traversed by no man-beast, only the descendants of Fatinah and Ali.

"Here we will begin the first route, like the way of the salt caravans from Bilma." With joy I lifted my head to the brilliance of the sun. "We need only explore!"

"What are we waiting for?" Seid pranced at the edge of the salt pan. "I want to know it all, this very moment!"

Thirteen

Many were the mysteries of our new world. Nearly four moons into the Mojave we wandered upon a place so strange . . .

"Oh," gasped Fatinah. "Is it the moon?"

"Ho," chorted Seid. "The moon is yellow! And this is—"

"What the moon might be like, could we visit it in the night sky," I said.

Vast slabs of stone—red as the setting sun, orange as a sweet root, white as the sand, and green as fine cattle grass—all tilted at one another like colossal bull camels in combat. And this battle seemed to go on about us forever. It silenced even Seid. But not for long.

"Father!" he yelped. His eyes had descended from the cliffs to the dry streambeds through which we ambled, all three of us gaping like the foreign Infidels had done during their rides into the Valley of the Kings. "Father! Stop and look!"

I lowered my eyes. "What is it?"

"A bone. A giant bone! I wonder, is it good to eat?"

In the Mojave our son had picked up an odd taste for bones. He was especially fond of antelope, claiming that the marrow inside a fresh leg bone was delicious. I myself could not understand these cannibalistic tendencies. I felt only relief that Seid still greeted the occasional small herd of these animals with courtesy and did not appear to have any but a normal interest in them while they were alive.

Fatinah gave our son an exasperated glance. "Really . . ."

Seid blithely ignored her. His teeth gnawed at a sharp pointed edge that looked almost like a horn. Then he spat. "It's rock, Father! Nothing but hard, disgusting rock. How can a bone turn into rock?"

I pawed at the bone, then at the others spread out neatly in a pattern nearby. The arrangement looked something like my friend Seid's bones after they'd dug them up and cleaned them before shipping them to Washington City. Only these were much, much larger. Ten times larger. "This was a creature of awesome size, son."

Fatinah nodded nervously toward the landscape around us. "Could there be others? Others who still live in this land of giants?"

I prodded my family away from the skeleton. "I think not. I think they have been gone for much longer than we have lived. Maybe longer even than before the Ancients. What else but the passing of millions of moons could change these bones to stone?"

We named the place the Land of Giants. Seid was always pressing us to return to that particular route, but Fatinah was not eager to, especially at the present time. Once again she was with young. Her condition made her skittish, even though her delivery was not yet near.

The wonders of our new home continued to delight us. Since my milk days I had longed to see and learn more of the world Allah had created. In our Mojave He did not disappoint me. Together, my family and I could explore the marvels of the desert as we wished. We could break enough trails to content even me—without men-beasts to lead us by the nose.

This made our discoveries all the richer.

Among these discoveries were new things to eat too: moist tubers inches below the hard ground that we could paw free; cactus that masqueraded as small spiny creatures but held honeyed juices within; flowers that bloomed only at night, offering up their rose-scented petals for nibbling under the moonlight. For these things I had no names. Hi-Jolly and the soldier-beasts were not in the Mojave to label them.

Several days after we'd left the Land of Giants, we discovered other bones. This time the bones were those of humans, and they were nearly as hard as those of the giants. Perhaps men-beasts and giants once lived together. I pushed my son away from the remains.

"It is not proper. Let them have their peace."

"I wasn't going to chew them, Father! I

know better than that. I was digging for what I saw beyond."

I looked past him into the small cave that sheltered the bones. He was right. There were objects. I nosed out one.

"What is it, Ali?"

"A kind of bowl, Fatinah. Like Hi-Jolly takes his nourishment from. But chipped from stone. And implements of some kind. Nothing of danger to us."

So we meandered on, nibbling at the creosote and saltbush; catching sight of solitary, scattered sheep with wonderful, curved horns such as I had never seen; running after the long-eared jackrabbits for sport; running from the rattlesnakes, the only creature of the desert that could do us harm.

Truly I believed the rattlesnakes to be our only danger in this Mojave until, one day, I paused from grazing to study the sky.

Enormous black clouds such as I had never witnessed were forming over us. Quickly forming. I turned to my family. "There will be rain soon." My son scoffed. "That's silly, Father. In our desert?" Then he looked up at the sky.

"Wow!"

In mere seconds the blackness had intensified. Fatinah gave a whinny of fright.

"Fast!" I ordered. "Out of this dry streambed. To that bluff! Run!"

"But, Father. It never rains in the desert, else why would it be so dry?"

"Don't argue. Follow me!"

I sprinted for the bluff, Fatinah following me. Seid held back, his nose still pointing at the sky—daring the heavens to rain when it was an impossibility. With Fatinah safe on high ground, I turned around as the first heavy drops of moisture hit my nose. Where was that young idiot?

"Wait here, Fatinah. Do not, for the love of Allah, move a toe-space lower. I will fetch our son. He'll receive more than a tongue-lashing for his disobedience."

As I edged down the steep incline, the rain fell colder and harder than any I'd ever experienced. Before my eyes the dry streambed on which we'd walked was filling. Overflowing. What had become of my son?

"Seid!" I bellowed. "Seid!"

I heard a whimpered answer, whirled, and saw him on the edge of the expanding stream, his feet stuck in the new mud that Allah had never designed us to handle. I did not waste my voice further but rushed through the now-raging river. Stepping carefully behind Seid, I pushed him with all my might. I could feel him shivering. Finally heard his feet sucked free from the muck.

"Run! For Allah's sake and that of your mother. Run for the bluff!"

He heaved himself against the rain as he strained to run. He managed at least to walk, with me behind, prodding. At the foot of the bluff, I shoved him on his way and struggled after him. Only just in time. Flashes of fire and thunder came out of the black sky, cutting through the sheets of water. I gasped at what I saw at my heels.

A very ocean was creeping up behind me. It was rising by the moment! I scrambled behind young Seid, the water licking my legs, until we reached the top and Fatinah.

She rushed to us, trembling with fear. "Praise Allah! You are both safe!" She nosed me and then our son, stopping the caress in midact. "Why? Why did you not obey your father instantly? For shame! You were almost destroyed!"

Seid's head fell in embarrassment. "Forgive me, Mother. Forgive me, Father. It won't happen again."

I tried to frown as sternly as possible. It didn't work. I ended up licking his face too. Then we stood watching the water rise till it came to our very knees. Quite suddenly—as suddenly as the storm had begun—it ended. The hot sun returned. The water receded before our disbelieving eyes.

"It is good to know," I spoke aloud thoughtfully. "The snake is not our only enemy here. But I believe we shall see rattlers many more times than a storm like this one."

The next few days were extraordinary in their beauty. Flowers I had neither imagined nor tasted bloomed. Strange little frogs and shelled creatures appeared in remaining pools of the washes. Seid amused himself by trying to catch these oddities but only ended with scratches upon his nose from tiny, sharp claws.

We followed the line of the water until

it vanished, swallowed once more by the desert sands, as if the storm had never happened. Several days beyond, we wandered into a rare canyon of more permanent beauty. There were many cliffs of great color, cut by the constant winds. But the best surprise was the river flowing beneath them. By some miracle it was a river the desert did not alter. Along its verdant banks grew healthy trees of tasty leaves and grasses that we sampled for old times' sake. Moved by wonder, I turned to Fatinah.

"This is a valley of true grace and innocence. We will call it Tito's Place, in his honor." My family nodded in approval.

"Wouldn't this be perfect for the birth of our new young one?" I asked.

Fatinah stopped grazing to consider. "It has beauty, yes. But this child . . . Somehow I should like this child to meet life in a spot more like home. I cannot explain it, Ali, but it is something I hunger for."

My brow furrowed in thought. "You mean the sand, Fatinah."

"Yes. The dunes. I feel they are near."

I gazed in the direction from which the sun rose. "They will be to the east. It is only logical. We'll rest a few days, then go to find them."

Because of Fatinah's condition, we moved slowly. The journey took more than a week. But several days before we arrived, I could smell sand on the wind.

As we neared the dunes, Seid could not hold himself back any longer. He bounded ahead of us at a gallop and disappeared over a rise. His scream of delight rode the wind back to us. Fatinah and I glanced at each other and broke into a lope.

It was true. Over the rise were *dunes*. *Sand dunes* as far as the eye could see. In his excitement, young Seid scrambled up the first, then slid down again, forgetting all the lessons he'd been taught. I skidded to a halt before the dune and watched him blow sand from his nose and mouth.

"Well?"

"At last! It's as wonderful as you said, Father! *Wheee!*" He scrambled to the top again, rolling in the sand in a delirium of ecstasy.

As Fatinah joined me, my excitement exploded. Were these not like the very dunes my father had raced across in my native land? Soon I was rolling alongside my son, with Fatinah beside us. I bellowed out a huge roar of pleasure at having finally found my heart's desire. Seid echoed it, and our roars sped up and down the dunes.

It was only when I heard Fatinah's bellow that I knew something about it was different. I rolled over once more and struggled to my feet.

"What is it, my Desert Flower?"

"The new baby, Ali. I was right . . ."

Seid glanced up with interest. "What's happening?"

"Play over on the next dune, son. Your mother needs to be alone."

Yasmin arrived by the light of the moon, as young Seid had. She was lovely. As lovely as her mother. This time I did not frighten the little one by bellowing into her ear. Instead, I moved off to a distant dune and sang my thanks to Allah and the stars. Was any camel in the East or West more fortunate than I?

Fourteen

Other adventures overtook us during our time in the desert. Many, many adventures. Possibly the most singular was the time we rounded a rocky butte one afternoon and sensed the almost forgotten smell of a man-beast. I pulled up short and motioned for my family to stay back in the lengthening shadows. Alone, I crept forward to learn what danger this might portend for us.

First, I heard the steady chipping sound of tools against hard rock. Next, I heard the unmistakable bray of a mule, agitated by my odor. I proceeded with less caution, knowing the mule would be tethered. I, at least, could run.

I stopped at the sight before me. A small camp was spread out beneath the sun: a mussed sleeping roll, dying embers of a fire, leather bags of supplies. But that was not what made my breath catch within me. It was the sight of the man-beast digging into the rock of the butte. For this was a man-beast I could never forget.

"Hi-Jolly!" I roared my greeting, and he dropped his tools to stare.

"By Allah." He squinted into the brightness. "It can't be! Ali? Is it truly you?"

He clambered over rubble, as small and skinny as when we first met but with more years upon his back. He stretched for my neck, and his eyes dropped tears in his excitement.

"Ali. Ali. You have found your desert! And I, too . . . but no gold. At least, little. Not El Dorado, not the Golden Mountain. But still I search." He ended his embrace and stepped back to admire me. "The years have been good to you, Ali. You prosper."

At that I had to beckon my family to prove how truly I had prospered. They came forth cautiously. Hi-Jolly's eyes widened. "It must be Fatinah, still with her Indian beads. And your son, fully grown. What's this? A daughter too?"

He reached for Yasmin, but never having received the touch of a man-beast, she shied away.

Hi-Jolly laughed. "You make me home-sick, Ali. No, not for the old country. That is too long gone. But for my wife and my own lovely daughters. The woman left me, Ali. Took the girls and went away. She said *gold* was more important to me than *they* were."

He rubbed at his scruffy chin. "Who knows? Perhaps she spoke truly. But still, a man feels need of company at times. In the desert, with no one but a stupid mule . . ."

Hi-Jolly sighed deeply, then began to rummage in his bags. "Here. For the sake of old times. I have a few dried apples left. Soon I must return to civilization for more supplies. There will be enough gold dust to buy more. Barely."

He offered the delicacy to me. I accepted it graciously, in the manner in which it was offered. Fatinah and Seid did the same. Hi-Jolly had to leave his gift for Yasmin on a nearby rock. Waiting till he was safely distant from her, she inched up to it. She tasted. I waited for the look of astonishment in her eyes. It came.

"Such sweetness, Father! I have never tasted such sweetness!"

I smiled and thanked Hi-Jolly for his

hospitality. Then, my family and I slowly ambled away, leaving him to watch us disappear into the distance.

Time slipped by. Allah in His wisdom took Fatinah from me. My children grew and went in search of their own paths. While I . . . I slowly became old as the Ancients. My wish for freedom had long since come to pass, but it no longer shone for me. What good was it to race free—like the wind, like my father—without companions? What good to roam in solitary splendor the many routes I had devised across this trackless land?

My victory had become bittersweet. Would I ramble this desert alone for the rest of my days? Was freedom—to be one with the sand and the wind—enough to fill my emptiness? Such had been my thoughts through many hot days and chilling desert nights—until I met Hi-Jolly once more.

Our meeting may have been fated for always, ordained by Allah. It was a hundred moons later, near another cliff, in another part of the Mojave.

This time Hi-Jolly did not offer me a sweet root or apple. Neither did he chip at the rock for his precious gold. Instead, he lay on his bedroll, staring into the hot sky.

His scent brought me to him. When I lowered my nose to his face, he blinked.

"Ali."

The word was acceptance.

"Ali. This is a strange land after all. The gold is never enough . . . never enough. . . . Even the desert becomes bitter."

My tongue tasted his salty face, gently. He closed his eyes. Was my old friend going to the Gardens of Heaven at last?

I raised my head. Through lashes burned by the desert sun, I studied afresh the land around me. Heat baked my neck and hump. It shimmered visibly, adding layers to the air. Slowly the layers parted, and I saw the Mother of All Rivers once more. It was before me, a shining ribbon dotted with feluccas and edged with palm. The Temple of Amun-Re, glittering with whiteness, was behind me; my mother stood at my side. What wisdom had I missed in my quest for freedom? What knowledge that could help me understand my mourning for this man-beast?

The layers dissolved, as all mirages must.

I bent my head for a final lick of Hi-Jolly's face. To my immense surprise, his eyes opened again. He raised his head weakly. Could it be? Could his time not truly be upon him?

I glanced around his campsite and spied something that might help. A water bottle! Maybe Hi-Jolly had lain under the treacherous sun too long. He did not have a hump to sustain him, after all. My teeth reached for the leathern strap, and I set the bottle upon his chest.

He smiled and fumbled with the cork. Soon life-saving water was trickling down his throat. I shaded his body with my own while he drank, then nudged him to a sitting position.

"Thank Allah!" he finally said. "It must have been a heat stroke. And you, Ali, have saved me! For see, my mule has deserted me. My supplies are gone." He drank again, then stared up at me.

"Could you forsake your desert for just a little time, Ali? Could you forsake your freedom? For just a little while to rescue an old friend?"

I backed off a few paces. What was being asked of me? And could I do it? I digested my thoughts, spitting them from my mouth as I had the shipboard donkey food so long ago. Hi-Jolly's words brought everything back to me. Our adventures, our comradeship.

Slowly it came to me that there was another path to be taken, another route to blaze. At last I remembered other words once spoken by my mother. Wise words about our destiny being tied to that of human-kind.

I returned to Hi-Jolly and lowered myself to him. He gratefully pulled himself onto my back. I set my pace to his rhythm as he began to sing with joy—softly at first, then with fresh vigor. Hi-Jolly's hand I would never need to bite. But should I find others that deserved it . . . the crunch and taste of salt would be even sweeter after all this time.

We headed West to the land of men.

Author's Note

The United States Camel Corps was a short-lived experiment by Secretary of War Jefferson Davis and the U.S. Army. A shipload of camels was brought to America from Egypt in 1856, and another in 1857. The camels were trained in Texas with hopes that they would solve the problems of an army trying to cope with desert terrain. Hi-Jolly, Major Wayne, Uncle Sam, Edward F. Beale, and a few other minor characters actually existed, although they have been partially fictionalized for this story.

The outbreak of the Civil War ended the experiment, and the rapid westward expansion of the railroad after the Civil War further eroded the need for camels. The remaining animals were either sold to mines and circuses, escaped, or were set free to fend for themselves. Camel sightings in the southwestern desert were still being made as late as the 1920s.

Edward F. Beale (1822-1893) was enthusiastic about camels, even learning Arabic so he could speak to them. He was especially fond of his camel, Seid. On the animal's death, he had its body exhumed and sent to the Smithsonian Institution in Washington, D.C., for scientific studies. Today Seid's skeleton is displayed in the

Smithsonian's Museum of Natural History.

Hi-Jolly (1828-1902) spent thirty years as a civilian employee of the army. After the Camel Corps was disbanded, he was a camel messenger for the California Volunteers during the Civil War. He learned Spanish and Indian dialects and was an army scout in the Apache Wars. He spent his later years prospecting for gold and died—alone and penniless—near Quartzsite, Arizona. His lonely burial site is marked by a pyramid of rocks topped with the silhouette of a camel.

For backgound on the Camel Corps, I studied the original documents held by the National Archives and Records Administration in Washington, D. C. Elegant period script filled the "Daily Journal kept on the Camel Deck, U.S. Ship Supply," by D.D. Porter Esq., Lieut. Commander. Major Henry C. Wayne, U.S. Army, offered "Notes upon the dromedaries met with in Egypt." The original correspondence of Jefferson Davis gave fascinating insights into the purchase of and hopeful plans for these animals. For the habits of camels themselves, I studied the resident occupants of the National Zoo, picked their keepers' brains, and was given gracious access to the Zoo's study library. To complete my research, I also rode camels on the sand dunes of both Egypt and Morocco. And they still intrigue me!

—Kathleen Karr